LEGACY

A Goodbye in the Keys

T.C. RYAN

ISBN 978-1-64300-976-6 (Paperback)
ISBN 978-1-64300-977-3 (Digital)

Covenant Books, Inc.
11661 Hwy 707
Murrells Inlet, SC 29576
www.covenantbooks.com

chapter
1

Claire sat on the rooftop deck overlooking the ocean. An early morning breeze breaking the heat of dawn's sun bristled across her cheek. This is her favorite time of the day, sipping a tall cup of coffee, meditating, listening to God through the waves crashing on the beach below. She planned her day and reflected on the blessings of the previous day.

She thought about how different her life was twenty years ago. She had worked hard, went back to school after she had kids to become a nurse. She always felt hospice was a calling and while she loved every minute of her career, she was also glad that she didn't have to maintain the daily grind. Of course, she never anticipated being a widow at sixty and always joked she would be paying off student loans with her Social Security. She and her husband always put off traveling until they had more money and thought they had plenty of time once they retired. She always assumed that since she was older, she would be the one to go first, but God had other plans. His death five years ago changed her. It taught her not to put off her dreams and to live in the present. Although she still grieved a little every day, she also knew that Dirk would want her to still be active and not wallow in pity. While she would give anything to have him back, she was also grateful for her current circumstances—she felt truly at peace for the first time in years. She made sure to give thanks daily and never took for granted the struggles, grief, and heartbreaks that brought her here.

She felt wet fur on her legs as her massive bulldog plopped down at her feet. She noted the boats on the nearby dock were starting up and beginning to be packed and brought to life for a day of work, fishing, or play. Her tranquility was over for the time being, and Tank gave her a hungry look. She got up, deciding it was time to get busy herself. She fed the dog, dove into the pool, feeling the shock of the cold water, and did a round of morning exercises. Tank lingered poolside, giving her intermingling looks of curiosity and boredom.

She had heard her phone ring multiple times which she had ignored. She knew by the ringtone, it was her friend Marcy. She also knew Marcy wouldn't give up trying to reach her until she either called back or answered directly. She gave the phone an evil smile as she turned it to vibrate until she could jump in the shower and get dressed. Marcy would always say it was an emergency, but it never really was. She was energetic, dynamic, and impossible to ignore for long. Once she had prepared herself for the conversation, she turned the ringer back on and was surprised to find that Marcy had left a voice mail which she rarely did. "Claire! Pick up your dadgum phone and call me back ASAP! You won't believe what I have to tell you!"

Just as she was finishing listening to the message, the doorbell rang, and someone was pounding on the door simultaneously. Marcy burst through the door, almost running her over as she opened it. "Why don't you ever answer your phone before 7:00 a.m.? What if one of your girls or grandkids needed you. What if it really was an emergency? What if I were lying dead in my apartment of a heart attack because you wouldn't answer your phone?" She didn't give Claire time to answer before she started in again, "Anyway, pack a bag. We are going on an adventure."

"What kind of adventure do you have planned this time?" Claire asked.

"Well, really, it's an adventure for me. More like work for you, but it will be good, I promise. Whisper's boss asked her to call me and see if you would be interested in a nursing gig in Key West. It is a private nursing gig of some sort. Before you say no, it would be good for you to work once in a while. You were a good hospice nurse and could use some diversion. I know this time of the year is hard for you. Come on, it'll be fun and besides... I know you have megabucks, but I don't. I could use the money since my Social Security doesn't kick in for another five years. My nest egg is getting moldy from all our travels."

Claire waited to see if Marcy would start in again before she responded. "First off, I'm not sure I really want to go back to work, and secondly, how is it money for you if I am the one doing the work? Last time I checked, you didn't have a current nursing license."

"I don't, but since it's been awhile, I thought I could be your assistant. You know, take care of Tank, do your shopping, laundry, be your personal secretary. Don't worry though, I'm not *that* expensive. And besides, you might enjoy the company of someone you know since we have to live there for the assignment, and your life would be so lonely without me. Just call Whisper and get the details." Whisper was Marcy's youngest daughter who worked for a lawyer that Claire knew well. Before Claire could object, Marcy already had Whisper dialed and handed the phone to Claire.

"Hi, Mom, any news?" Claire heard and grabbed the phone.

"Hi, Whisper, it's actually Claire. Your mom said you wanted to talk to me about a job?"

"Oh, hi, Claire. Yes, I did. Can you take me off speaker?" Claire obliged, and Whisper continued, "Have you ever heard of Brian Montgomery?"

"Of course, he is a celebrity. I have seen a couple of his movies. Is he the patient?"

"I can't really give you more information until you sign a confidentiality agreement. Can you come by the office?"

"I can check my calendar and get back to you tomorrow if that would work." Claire was hesitant.

"Actually, I was hoping you could come by in an hour or so? I can get a contract ready for you to examine and give you all the details then. I promise, this is right up your alley, and the pay is generous. It is definitely worth your while to check it out."

"An hour? Is it really that urgent?"

"I'm afraid so. He is really insistent we get the process moving as quickly as possible, so I'll see you in an hour, okay?"

Whisper hung up before Claire could protest. She handed the phone back to Marcy who was grinning from ear to ear.

"Traffic was heavy on the way here, so maybe we should leave now." Marcy was literally dancing a little jig on her way back out the door.

Whisper was on the phone but saw them come in and waved them over to her desk. Whisper was a younger mirror image of her mother but with a stressed, tired look that had Claire a little concerned. She had the same colorful taste in clothes as Marcy but Whisper's was a more professional and polished look. While Marcy's hair had turquoise streaks in it this week, Whisper's was a deep mahogany with streaks of purple. They both had the same mesmerizing green eyes, beautiful olive skin, thick eyelashes that required no mascara, and dazzling smiles. "She is here now, Mr. Montgomery. I should have the contract signed and faxed to you this afternoon. I will call you when everything is finalized and give you a time of arrival." She waived Claire and Marcy into a conference room while the caller was obviously talking. "Yes sir," she answered, "I will call you back in an hour or so."

She hung up the phone and followed them into the conference room. She gave Claire and Marcy hugs and pulled up the chair beside them. "Thank you so much for coming in so quickly, Claire. I know this seems like a lot, and you are doing me and my boss a huge favor. We really appreciate you at least looking at this and considering it."

"I understand you are in a bind, Whisper, but I haven't had time to really consider this yet. I haven't said yes, and I really am hesitant about rushing into this," Claire warned. "Where is the confidentiality agreement so I can sign it and get more details?"

"I have it right here along with the contract." Whisper slid the one-page document over and pulled out the contract which she handed to Claire once the first document was signed. "I will give you a few minutes to look the contract over while I keep Mother occupied and have her sign a confidentiality agreement as well.

"Good luck with that one." Claire chuckled. Whisper took Marcy's hand and said, "Come on, Mom. Let's go make some tea."

"You girls are no fun." Marcy huffed as they walked out of the room.

6

It was a standard contract in many ways. Mr. Montgomery was diagnosed with stage IV cancer, and his doctor recommended a private-duty nurse if he wanted to remain at home. Lodging, food, and basic necessities were provided along with $20,000 per month for 24/7 on-call duty until her services were no longer required. It was a huge sum of money and benefits. Claire couldn't help but wonder what the catch was. Claire would work directly with Mr. Montgomery's oncologist for medication orders and treatment management. They would be lodged in a guesthouse on the Montgomery compound, and Claire could bring Tank and Marcy with her. She finished reading all the fine print and noted Whisper was quietly standing in the corner when she looked up.

"For that kind of money, he could hire anyone. Why me?" Claire asked.

"Simple," Whisper answered. "Because we could get you quickly, and you don't have a lot of loose ends to tie up before you can start. He was made aware of your semi-retirement and was impressed with your resume, which I supplied without your permission and apologize for that. I just knew you would be perfect for the job." Whisper blushed.

Claire laughed. "Where did you find a resume of mine? I haven't done one in years!"

"You had an old copy on a career site, I copied it and updated it with your current address and last job. I can be resourceful if I have to be." Whisper strutted just a little. "Plus you are grounded, more mature, and won't be star struck like a newer nurse would be. Although, keeping Mother out of the way while you work might be challenging and worth that paycheck."

They both chuckled. "Mr. Montgomery knows he is getting sicker by the day and fears he has waited too long to ask for help. He thought he could get away with just having his employees on the compound manage his treatment but realized that he really needs someone with more medical knowledge."

Claire sighed. "I just don't know if I am up for this challenge, Whisper. It's been almost five years since I've worked in nursing. How about if I agree to go down and get a feel of the situation? I will work with him until you can come up with a backup plan if I don't feel comfortable," Claire suggested.

"Deal," Whisper squealed as she hugged Claire tightly. "I know you haven't worked since Dirk died, but I really feel this assignment is perfect for you, or at least it's perfect for Mr. Montgomery. I will go gather all the medical records and background information you will need, then call him back and let him know you will leave today and be there later tonight. I can't tell you how much I appreciate this, Claire." Whisper turned and gave a thumbs up to Marcy who was peering through the glass.

Marcy responded by raising her hands in the air, dancing in a little circle and yelling "Woohoo" a little louder than the other office staff appreciated.

Marcy talked nonstop on the way back to her condo while Claire sat, wondering what had she gotten herself into. Claire took a deep breath before walking into Marcy's house. While Marcy wasn't particularly messy, she was cluttered and a collector almost to the hoarder status. Enough so that Claire had to zigzag through a narrow path and felt almost claustrophobic in the small living room. The advantage was that the condo had a lovely balcony that had a breathtaking view of the beach which was where Claire headed. Marcy's furniture had its own style. Some pieces were beautiful antiques that seemed out of place while others were fascinating, and some of the pieces were just strange in Claire's opinion. They came from all over the world, and there were some Claire had helped pick out during their travels together.

"Make yourself at home," Marcy yelled from the other room. "I'll only be a few minutes. How long do I need to pack for?"

"They have a washer and dryer available," Claire said. "Just pack for a couple of weeks and try to keep it light."

Claire walked onto the balcony, leaned over the rail, and whispered a silent prayer, "Lord, please, get me through this."

chapter
2

Once both were packed and houses locked up for the undetermined time, they were on the road. Claire's housekeeper, Maria, was in charge of all the duties while they were away. Just like their previous trips, Claire was responsible for coordinating it all. Luckily, Maria didn't mind and was accustomed to dealing with it all. The only downside was that they usually had more time to plan. Regardless, they all worked quickly, and the two were on the road before noon. Normally the traffic through the Keys was heavy and could take all day, but the heavens were on their side, and they actually made fairly good time. Marcy alternated between singing, talking incessantly, or heckling other drivers. Claire knew it was better not to concentrate on Marcy's driving and stuck to reviewing her new patient's medical history, scan results, and a summary of doctor recommendations included in the large packet Whisper provided.

Claire also noted that Whisper included a personal history which the lawyer had prepared from previous dealings with Mr. Montgomery. The lawyer assembled a much more professional dossier that gave a very different perception of Brian Montgomery than the general public knew. Claire found it interesting and very helpful. However, Marcy relied on information provided by the gossip magazines. Claire made a thorough list of questions to ask Montgomery's doctor.

"You do realize that over half the info you gave me from those gossip rags is garbage, don't you, Marcy?"

"Not true!" Marcy snapped, "it's not like I gave you the *Country Inquisitor*. I gave you the more reputable magazines. They check their sources! Although I am sure celebrities aren't always truthful in interviews, but Oprah and Barbara Walters don't lie, and those articles match up with interviews I have seen with them."

"That's exactly my point! Celebrities say stuff in those interviews that they think the public wants to hear. Would you tell a million strangers the truth about your life? Never mind, you probably would. The point is, celebrities will say what they need to so they can sell a movie, magazine, or book they are promoting." Claire argued.

"Well, maybe you're right, but you just burst a bubble of mine, so let me use my imagination a little, will ya? I hate to think my favorite movie stars lead boring lives like mine."

"Marcy, our lives are not boring. But I am sure many of the people you borderline idolize are just ordinary ol' people that aren't that much different than you or me. We all put our pants on one leg at a time. I am sure Mr. Montgomery will tell you some things about himself, but I want you to remember your confidentiality agreement and not spread any gossip, rumors, or talk to anyone about anything that takes place while we are there. You do understand that, don't you?"

"Oh, I guess I really didn't think about it. I didn't read that stupid paper, I just signed it so I could come along. How am I supposed to keep all this stuff secret?" Marcy truly looked deflated. "I was hoping to be the envy of my painting class. I may actually burst if I have to keep all this fun to myself!"

"I don't think that is actually possible, dear friend. Anytime you think of opening your mouth, I want you to picture him or his lawyer suing your pants off and losing everything you own. Please, tell me I can trust you, or I will have you drop me off and have you turn around and take Tank home with you."

"No, no! I promise. I don't like it one little bit, but I promise. Man! You know how to ruin a beautiful drive and turn all my excitement into stress, don't you?"

"I'm sorry, Marcy. I really am, but I feel like it is also my job to protect you. I don't want to see you in trouble!"

"Hmpphh! Trouble used to be my middle name until I started hanging out with you." Marcy pouted. They slowed and looked around. The navigation system told them that they had arrived at their destination, but there was nothing in the street. No houses, no buildings—only very tall hedges that were a little unusual this far South, but they lined the streets the past mile.

"Stupid navigator has us stranded in the middle of nowhere! You should hop out, Claire, and see if you can see anything between those hedges."

Claire started to open her door when a black Jaguar pulled up beside them and rolled down the passenger window. An older, distinguished gentleman leaned over and motioned for Marcy to roll down her window. Marcy was hesitant. A lonely street and a complete stranger—even though the car was high-end and gorgeous, a girl just couldn't be safe nowadays. The gentleman waited patiently, realizing their predicament.

"My gun is in the glove box, Claire. Be prepared to grab it," Marcy said seriously as she inched down the window.

"Mrs. Sinclair and Mrs. Roberts?" the gentleman asked. "Don't be afraid! My name is Gerard, and I work for Mr. Montgomery. I am to lead you to the house. You don't have to get out of the car, just follow me, please."

Both Marcy and Claire breathed a sigh of relief as Marcy rolled up the window. "Get the gun out just in case. You can never be too careful!"

Suddenly the giant hedge in front of them opened up. "What an amazing gate!" Marcy cried out, and Claire agreed.

"It is definitely a beautiful fence too!"

The drive was over a mile long, and several small houses scattered throughout the landscape, all built in the common Key West style with balconies and beautifully large front porches. Claire counted six in all, and each had a pool varying in size. The main house was massive and not what either of them expected. It resembled a structure right out of *Gone with the Wind*.

"Wowsa!" Marcy exclaimed. "Not what I expected! I expected sleek and modern and all glass."

"I hate to admit it, but I did too," Claire chimed in.

The landscaping was immaculate and beautiful with large stone structures, fountains, hedges, and a beautiful courtyard with a large fountain and all types of tropical flowers. Marcy said she counted at least thirty large fruit trees on the drive in. The entire compound was elegant, simple, rustic, and very inviting.

Gerard led them to one of the larger of the guesthouses and helped them unload their bags. "Sorry, ladies, I didn't mean to scare you back there. I should have thought to bring my wife with me."

Marcy laughed. "A few more seconds and that beautiful Jaguar would have been riddled with bullet holes."

"I wouldn't have been concerned. It is bulletproof," Gerard stated impassively.

Marcy and Claire each shot the other a look with raised eyebrows. The guesthouse was approximately three thousand square feet by Claire's estimation and included a lovely screened in back patio that held an Olympic-sized salt water pool, four generous-sized bedrooms, and three bathrooms. It was all tastefully decorated with coastal-style furniture, and the rooms were all brightly painted yellow or blue. The kitchen was quite large for the style of house, and Marcy couldn't wait to explore. Tank sniffed around for a few minutes and plopped himself down in front of the French doors going out to the patio.

Marcy stood in the breakfast nook, dropped her bag and gazed, mouth open, out into the nearby courtyard. It was rare for Claire to see her friend speechless and while the compound was beautiful, it was not exactly Marcy's style. Claire followed Marcy's gaze and saw what had her friend so dumbfounded. There was a well-built man doing yoga in all his natural glory. Claire couldn't help but giggle softly—not from the naked man, but her friend was practically drooling. Gerard glanced over where Marcy was staring, cleared his throat, and stood in front of Marcy. "May I give you a small tour, Mrs. Sinclair?"

"Well, I was definitely enjoying the view, Gerard. Has anyone told you that you make a better door than a window?" Marcy joked.

Completely ignoring her remarks, Gerard guided her by the elbow into the kitchen. "I apologize that I did not have time to compile a list of your dietary requests, but my wife and I stocked enough supplies in the pantry and refrigerator until you can give us a more complete list. I expect to head back into town in the next few days."

"I am sure it will be fine, Gerard. We greatly appreciate it," Claire said. She picked up her luggage and turned around. "I assume the bedrooms are this way?"

"Yes, ma'am. There are two back bedrooms with lovely views of the grounds if you prefer, or the two upper bedrooms offer plenty of shade from the surrounding trees. Please choose which you prefer. I will leave you to get settled and hope that you will join us all in the main house for dinner."

"That would be lovely, thank you. I take it we will meet our gracious host at dinner?" Claire asked.

"Yes, Mrs. Roberts. Mr. Montgomery will be joining us for dinner."

"Again, thank you for everything. And Gerard, please call us Claire and Marcy. I expect we will be getting to know each other very well in the next few weeks."

"Yes, ma'am. Dinner should be ready around 7:00 p.m. and cocktails at 6:30 p.m. Will that be all right?"

"Perfect, Gerard," Marcy answered. "Although I prefer white wine, please. It's probably not a good idea to be plastered during our first meeting. Before you leave, how do you get such beautiful varieties of trees to grow here? These are not indigenous to Florida."

"The gardener has soil shipped from all over. He is a miracle worker with horticulture and maintains proper acid balance. I will give him your compliments." Gerard gave her a half-bow and left quietly out the back door.

chapter
3

Claire unpacked her bags and changed into her swimsuit. She thought a nice dip would help her stretch out after the long car ride. She went into the kitchen and found Marcy head first in the fridge, butt wiggling.

"Find anything interesting?"

"Holy frijole, Claire, I think I have died and gone to heaven. Will you look at these?" She pulled out two very large pies. Claire noted that one was a Key lime and the other looked like a French Silk. "Want me to cut you a piece?" Marcy asked.

"No thanks, not right now. I'm gonna take a quick dip and then shower before dinner."

"Man, you must have a will of steel. Ain't nothin' stopping me from diving into these beauties!" Marcy pulled out a plate and began cutting herself a very large piece of each pie.

"Try and save me a little and don't ruin your dinner." Claire smiled as she headed towards the pool. She could hear Marcy humming and licking her lips.

The pool felt refreshing, and Claire enjoyed stretching her legs. She got out after about twenty minutes. She found some dog bowls on the patio, grabbed them, and filled one up with water, adding some ice cubes to it. She looked in the pantry to see if there was anything she could feed Tank and found a small bag of kibble. She poured him a bowl, and he woofed it down in seconds. Marcy appeared with chocolate still on her cheek and a large spot of chocolate on her blouse.

"I take it the pie was good?" Claire smiled.

"It was *bellisimo*! You are lucky I saved you some. How was the pool?"

"Perfecto! Just what the doctor ordered. You want to take a shower first?" Claire hinted.

"Sure," Marcy replied. "You think dinner is going to be formal or informal?"

"I am guessing somewhere in between would be good. But when did you ever worry about dress code?"

"I guess I am just nervous about meeting a celebrity. Especially one with the body of a Greek God! I don't think I will get that image out of my mind for a very long time, although I am definitely not complaining." Marcy turned and headed towards her room.

Claire looked at the dog. "How about a walk after your dinner, Tank?" The dog just stood and stared at her, breathing hard, and drooling significantly. She grabbed his harness, a plastic bag for poo, and a rag to wipe his face with. They started out the front door, and Claire stopped and admired the scenery. Marcy was right. There were all kinds of fruit trees, palm trees, and stunning stone sculptures scattered throughout the compound.

Tank was in his own heaven, lifting his leg on everything they passed. He even broke out into a run and into a fountain, splashing like a puppy. He did his business, and they returned to the house.

Marcy was humming in her room, and Claire didn't hear the shower, so she assumed it was safe to jump in. Once ready, she grabbed her purse, then decided against taking it with her, but noticed her phone. She saw a text from Whisper. "Mr. Montgomery notified me of your arrival. Good luck, sounds like you may need it."

Claire sent a text back, saying, "How about a prayer? Might help more." She placed her phone on the bedside table and wondered how she got herself into these situations. "Lord, I know you are here with me but stick close, please. I have a feeling I will need you."

The massive door to the main house opened before they even knocked. Gerard and his wife waved them into the foyer. "Welcome, ladies. I would like to introduce you to my wife, Sable."

Sable extended her hand, and Marcy brushed it away opting for a massive bear-hug instead.

"Sable, I can't thank you enough for the delicacies you left for us. Those pies were absolutely to die for. Where did you buy them?"

Sable blushed a little. "The pies were the only things I had time to make myself. I'm glad you enjoyed them, Mrs. Sinclair. They are from my grandmother's recipes."

"Oh please, darling, you *must* give me those recipes! It took every ounce of willpower to save Claire a piece of each!"

"Thank you, ma'am. That means a lot to me," Sable spoke so softly. Sable reached out to shake Claire's hand and like Marcy, Claire chose a courteous hug, not quite as overwhelming as Marcy's—but sincere.

"Now where is that gorgeous hunk of a man I saw earlier! No offense, Gerard, but Mr. Montgomery is stunning!" Marcy winked. "And don't look so scared, Gerry, I know how to behave myself when I have to."

Gerard and Sable looked at each other worriedly and wondered if that was possible. Marcy fluffed her wild hair and looked at them. "Do I look all right?"

Marcy was dressed in a cross between a muumuu, a sundress, and a bathing suit cover up. It was a blinding red silk that had colorful parrots emblazoned throughout. She wore an ankle bracelet that resembled sandals winding around her ankles and toes but had no sole. Combined with her wild dark hair highlighted with turquoise, she looked as she had just jumped off a gypsy wagon. Claire was so accustomed to Marcy's style; she had become blind to the looks that Marcy often received when they went out in public.

"You look dazzling, ma'am." Sable smiled.

Claire was dressed in off-white linen Capri-length slacks with an aqua chemise and a matching sheer cover. When they entered the library, Brian Montgomery stood. They all surmised each other, and the three broke into laughter. He was dressed in long off-white linen shorts with a red cotton short-sleeve shirt that had parrots embroidered on it. He was a perfect mix of the two ladies.

Gerard made formal introductions, and Montgomery shook hands with the ladies and welcomed them.

"It is such an honor to meet you, Mr. Montgomery. I am a huge fan. I have seen all your movies and shows and have followed you for years. I must know the name of your plastic surgeon, you look so incredibly young." Marcy gushed.

"Thank you, Marcy. May I call you Marcy?" His rich baritone voice was soothing and slightly sarcastic, but Marcy didn't pay any heed and just kept going.

"Of course, I insist. I truly hope to have an opportunity to get to know you much better." She flirted.

17

He ignored her last statement and turned to Claire. "Welcome, Claire. Thank you so much for being available so quickly. It is a pleasure to meet you." He grabbed her hand and did a small bow as he kissed it.

Now it was Claire's turn to blush. "Thank you, Mr. Montgomery. You were lucky that I hadn't left for my yearly summer trip to Colorado to see my children."

"Please, call me Brian or Monty. I answer to both. Please, have a seat. Sable made some strawberry lemonade and fresh peach tea. I also have wine as you requested. Which do you prefer?"

"I will have the wine please, Monty," Marcy quipped, making sure to sit directly by her host.

"Thank you, Brian. I will have the lemonade. Sounds wonderfully refreshing on such a warm evening." Claire sat opposite Marcy and Montgomery.

Brian inched slightly away from Marcy as he turned to her. "Marcy, your daughter, Whisper, is quite impressive. She sounds lovely. I hope you will show me a picture so I can put a face to her voice." As Marcy pulled out her phone to find a picture, he asked, "How did you come up with such an unusual name for her?"

She handed him the phone and said, "Please don't let her know I showed you this one. It was taken on vacation several months ago, and she wasn't wearing makeup. I actually caught her first thing in the morning. She has a much nicer professional headshot, but I didn't bring my purse with me. She would shoot me if she knew I showed that one to you. As for her name, my husband and I were flower children and a little stuck in the late 60s. I also have a daughter named Sunshine, and my son Timber, but Timber was killed in a surfing accident with his father a long time ago."

"I'm so sorry for your loss." Brian sounded sincere, "I know how hard it must have been to raise your children alone. My mother was a single mom."

"Thank you, Monty. It was difficult, but I had a village, so my girls had plenty of support and love." She patted him on the knee and left her hand there, gently stroking his bare leg.

Brian ignored her hands and turned to Claire. "So, Claire, forgive me, but I do know a little about you. Before hiring any employee, I have to make sure and do a thorough background check. I am sorry for your loss as well. It was nice to see you got a handsome settlement from the bastard that did that to your husband."

Marcy interrupted, "That was thanks to Whisper and me insisting that her boss, Mr. Harper, take the case. Claire doesn't believe in lawsuits and fought us all the way. If it had been up to her, she would have forgiven that hideous monster."

Brian raised his eyebrows. "Really?"

Claire turned red and gave Marcy a glare. Brian sensed the tension, cleared his throat, and gracefully changed the subject. "Well, I hope you ladies are hungry. Sable just gave me the signal that our first course is ready. He stood and ushered them into a beautiful dining room that smelled of wood, leather, and campfire.

They sat at a very large custom-made wooden table. Various animal heads gave them vacant stares from every corner of the room. They were served a delicious, cold carrot squash soup, a spinach strawberry salad with a light avocado dressing.

Marcy talked nonstop throughout the meal, shooting questions at Montgomery as if she were interviewing him for one of those magazines she loved so much. After a while though, her questions became much more personal and bold for a first-time house guest, and Montgomery stiffened a little, turning more serious. He kept trying to dodge Marcy's questions and ask Claire questions, but Marcy would interrupt and fire off another series. He finally shot Marcy a stare, and she squirmed back a little, cheeks turning red. Not one to be so easily offended, she just switched the topic to herself and kept talking. By the time the main course of herbed salmon roulade was served, Montgomery stood up and excused himself.

After waiting a few awkward minutes for him to return, Claire looked over at Marcy and scolded, "I'm sorry, Marcy, but you really need to learn some self-control while we are here. He gets hounded every day by people, I am sure. Try to remember we are guests in his safe haven."

Marcy looked down at her plate. "I really should go apologize. I was more nervous than I thought, and I just can't control my mouth when I am nervous."

Gerard stepped into the room. "Ladies, I apologize, but Mr. Montgomery has taken ill and retired to his suite. He would like for you ladies to stay and finish your meal. Ms. Claire, he asks that you come upstairs to check on him before you leave."

"Oh, maybe we should leave now then," Marcy wondered.

"Please, stay and enjoy the rest of your dinner," Gerard said. "I know Sable so enjoys cooking and would be appreciative if you stayed."

"Only if you and Sable join us," interjected Claire. "It feels awkward in this big dining room with just the two of us."

"Thank you, Ms. Claire, but Sable and I enjoy eating in the sun room."

"Perfect, we will join you there," Marcy said as she began picking up plates and silverware. Realizing she was not taking no for an answer, Gerard and Claire started doing the same and joined Sable who was still eating her soup. Sable immediately jumped up, looking surprised as the two ladies sat down at the small patio table to join them. She gave Gerard an inquisitive look, and he stated, "Mr. Montgomery isn't feeling well and headed off to bed. The ladies didn't want to stay unless they could eat with us."

They finished their dinner together and just as Sable got up to bring out dessert, Claire got up and began clearing dishes.

"Please don't worry yourself, Mrs. Roberts. I can get those." Sable jumped up.

"I like doing dishes, Sable. Please sit with your husband and enjoy your dessert. I am technically not a guest. I am an employee just like you two. I would like to help do my part and then go see to Mr. Montgomery."

"You've done enough, ma'am. And we appreciate the thought. Let me show you to his room." Gerard stepped in.

They walked to the back of the kitchen, past the largest pantry Claire had ever seen, and she stopped abruptly.

"Is that a dumbwaiter? Does it work? I haven't seen one of those in years!"

"It is. Mr. Montgomery had it installed when he built the house several years ago. Initially it was so that we could send him up breakfast to his room without disturbing him when he was... entertaining."

Claire had to smile at Gerard's embarrassment. He quickly recovered and said, "It is a good thing, too, we have used it often since he began showing signs of his sickness."

chapter
5

They took a back stairway into a large hallway. There were two bedrooms on one side that had a Jack-and-Jill bath. On the other side of the hallway was a large bedroom with its own suite. A large double sliding barn door opened into the master bedroom. The bedroom itself was larger than her first studio apartment. Sitting in a recliner looking out to the ocean, Brian Montgomery was lightly sleeping. She pulled up an ottoman and sat beside him as Gerard headed back downstairs and closed the door behind her.

"Brian?" She lightly touched his arm. He opened his eyes slowly and took a moment to fully become alert.

"Hi, Claire. Sorry to be a miserable host and party pooper. I am sure Marcy will grow on me in time. I like her style, but I just couldn't take any more questions. I needed some quiet."

"I understand and apologize. I know she is very nervous and very excited to meet you. I promise to have a talk with her and keep her time with you directly limited."

"Thank you for that. I should warn you both that most of the time, I am an ass. I don't mean to be, but just ask Gerard. He usually gets the brunt of my fury. I know I have to behave myself so you will stay. I really don't want to die alone, and I have pushed everyone else out of my life. I have some conditions and questions for you. Are you up for it tonight?"

Claire was bone-tired, it had been a long day, but she decided she should hear what he had to say and decide if she should be prepared to find a hotel for tonight and head home in the morning. She took a deep breath and said, "Sure."

"Good. My first condition is that you keep your phone with you 24/7. You will not be expected to be at my side at all times, but I do expect you to be here quickly if I need you." He waited while Claire nodded her head. "At some point, I will want you to move in across the hall, not Marcy, but you. Also you should know that I have been to rehab several times for alcohol and heroine. I had been clean for ten years before I was diagnosed, and I am very hesitant about taking a lot of drugs now. I need to know that you will give me what I need only when I really need it. Do you have a problem with that?"

"I believe in the hospice philosophy of dying with dignity, making whatever time you have left the best quality time possible. I believe in pain management, but I will tell you that I am bound by doctor's orders. I cannot and will not put my license in jeopardy to accommodate you. I will always advocate for you and let the doctor know what I see and give him the clinical information he needs to make an informed decision. I have worked with addictions before and know when I am being manipulated, so as long as we are clear, then medication shouldn't be a problem."

"Okay." He was quiet for a moment. "I can respect that. Sable has been in charge of giving me medication, but she is very uncomfortable with it. So she will be relieved to have someone else take over. I don't trust myself, and I have a few demons to confront before I am ready to check out. Also Whisper told me that you are religious. I will probably offend you on a daily basis, and I don't want religion shoved down my throat, are you gonna be okay with that?"

"Brian, I have worked with people from all races, cultures, and religions. My job is to help you, how you believe is between you and God. I will always be honest with you and if you ask me questions, I will answer, but I will never initiate a spiritual conversation with you. As far as offending me, all I ask is that you treat me with respect, and I will do the same. As I said, anything you say or do is between you and God and has nothing to do with me."

"Fair enough. For the last few weeks, I get up around 8:00 a.m. and take my meds after breakfast, I do my yoga and then nap. I expect you to be here in the morning for my meds, and I want to know what I am taking. Neither Sable or I know what I take, she just hands me pills. We can talk more in the morning, but I am done for tonight, so please leave."

"What if I have questions for you?'

"Your friend took up that time, and I am not in the mood. So I would really just like you to leave."

She stood up and started to walk out the door but realized she was there to be a nurse, not a fan. So she turned around and walked back toward him. He didn't look happy that she did not follow orders and snipped. "What part of leave don't you understand?"

"You hired me as a nurse. I would like to do a quick exam. It won't take long, but I need to establish my own baseline. I am sorry, but I need to ask you questions while you are awake and able to answer."

"In the morning." He stood up and pointed at the door. She decided now was not the time to pick a fight and since she didn't bring her bag with her, she thought it best to not tick him off more than he already was.

"Good night, Mr. Montgomery." She left to go talk to Sable and refresh her memory of what drugs he was taking. She had the list in her packet in her room, but it was always better to check since some patients took over the counter medications or supplements that they didn't always tell their doctors about.

She spent an hour talking to Gerard and Sable, going through the medications and making notes to ask the doctor about the next morning. By the time she returned to her room, Marcy was already working on her third very large glass of wine and dozing while listening to her headset. She waved, and Marcy gave her a questioning look, but Claire just shook her head no and went to her room. She went through her nightly routine and fell asleep before her head even hit the pillow.

chapter
6

The next few days were busy getting into a schedule and getting to know one another. Sable and Marcy hit it off and were always in the kitchen laughing, singing, and cooking. Claire met with Brian's doctor and office nurse to work out a care plan and set up the logistics since she was not actually working with a company. Several times in the first two days, Brian would call her and ask her to come to his room immediately, then tell her he was just timing her when she went into his room. After the third time, Claire decided it was time to speak up.

"Brian, do you mind if we talk?"

"Let me guess, you are quitting. Have Gerard write a check for your time, and I will sign it."

"That's not it at all. But I would like to ask why you keep calling me in here just to tell me nothing is wrong. I appreciate the exercise but that type of behavior is only going to make me question every time you do call. Why are you afraid I won't come?"

"I don't know. I guess I am bored and am really hoping you will stay and just hang out."

"Then just say so. I can make phone calls and send my updates from in here if you would like. I just don't want to intrude when I have always gotten the sense you don't really want anyone around."

"That's just it, I really have always liked my solitude. When you have paparazzi following your every move for years, you become wary of everyone and tend to isolate yourself. The strange part is when the paparazzi isn't around, it feels like I don't matter anymore. I have pretended to be something that the public wants for so long,

I forgot how to just be myself. My staff probably tells you I'm an ass, sorry, a jerk. And I guess I am, but I don't really want to be. Gerard, Sable, and the staff here on the compound are the only people I know that have stood by me for more than a few weeks."

"That makes sense. I can't imagine what it would be like to never have time alone or having to put on a persona every day. When you are alone, what are the things you enjoy the most?"

"I guess I like doing my yoga but since you and Marcy arrived, I probably won't be doing that much. I prefer to do that in the nude. I also like reading scripts for possible projects, editing film, critiquing movies, working with sound mixers, that kind of stuff."

"Sounds like you love your job which is great. But other than yoga, what do you like doing that helps you relax?"

"I am always working. In this business, once you stop working, you are done, *finito*, forgotten. You have to be constantly thinking about the next project or deadline."

"Okay, name something you had to learn for a part or for work that you enjoyed. Like surfing, sailing, hiking, painting... anything like that?"

"I have a boat but only take it out when we have guests or entertaining. I obviously love the ocean, but I don't really spend much time *in* the water. Now, I don't feel like I have the energy for it anymore."

"How about you make a list of all the things you would really like to do, and maybe Gerard and I can come up with ways to accommodate them."

"Why would you do that for me when I have been a jerk to you?"

"You haven't been a jerk. Your actions are a normal reaction to grief. You are going to have good days and bad days ahead. Let's take advantage of the good days. There is nothing wrong with you reading scripts and making notes of how you would direct them if that is something you love, although if reading them would cause stress, then I wouldn't suggest it. You just need some diversions. I can always send Marcy up if you are missing the paparazzi you know," she said smiling.

Brian laughed. "She is entertaining for sure. Is she going to gawk if I do my yoga?"

"Probably, but I will have Sable find things to do for her at a certain time so she isn't near the courtyard. You could always try early morning too. She doesn't like to get up before 8:00 a.m. That's one reason why I get up early, I often have to distract her to get things done." She laughed.

"Thanks Claire. And thanks for not quitting. I will try to behave."

"Make your list. Consider it a bucket list, but I wouldn't advise traveling out of the country right now. While I am here, how about I do my assessment? How's your pain?" She stayed for another half an hour, and Brian seemed more relaxed when she left.

The next morning, she was slightly surprised when she got out of the pool at 6:00 a.m. to find Brian in the courtyard. Luckily, he was behind a bush, so she didn't see all of him. She chose to leave him in peace and ignored him as she started her own yoga routine. She must have been very deep in thought because she didn't even hear him but felt a presence behind her. When she looked back, she was grateful that he had on a pair of swim trunks.

"Good morning," he said. "I hope I am not interrupting your routine."

"You're fine, but just so you know, I don't chant or chatter when I do my yoga."

"Perfect, I will keep my inane banter to a minimum. But I noticed a couple of your moves that were interesting, would you mind showing me?"

She couldn't help but laugh. "I will bet that is the first time you ever asked for help with 'your moves.' Everything I learned, I learned from the senior center though. My yoga is more of a blend of Tai chi and yoga."

He smiled and even blushed a little. "Well, I haven't had any complaints about my moves and maybe the senior moves are just what I need right now." He smiled.

And she had to admit, he was charming when he wanted to be, but she sincerely hoped he wasn't flirting with her. That was the last thing she needed. He moved in a little too close for her comfort, and she backed away. She teasingly said, "Back away, buddy so I don't kick you by accident."

"You smell really good, you know. And I did find something on my bucket list that I am pretty good at, is relaxing, and you could help me with."

Claire stood up and backed up even farther. "Look, Brian, I am flattered if you are actually flirting with me but please know that I am not interested in anything but a friendship and professional relationship with you. Besides I am much older and not your type from what I can tell."

He looked a little dejected but shrugged his shoulders. "No sweat, your loss. But if you change your mind, let me know."

She continued with her routine and didn't even notice when he left just as silently as he had arrived. Two hours later, she was summoned to his room once again. "How was my time?" she quipped as she walked in only to find he was not in his usual chair. "Brian? Where are you?"

"In the bathroom," he replied in a weak voice. She walked in and found him naked in the shower on the floor. She turned off the water and reached down to help him stand. He grabbed her hand and pulled her down beside him. She panicked, screamed, and tried to get up, slipping on the wet floor.

"What are you doing?" she screamed.

"Trying to stand, I can't see—everything is spinning. I feel like I am going to puke."

She regained her footing and grabbed the trash can, thrusting it underneath him with only seconds to spare. When he was done, she reached for a washrag and helped him clean his mouth. "I am sorry you are sick but please don't ever grab me like that again. You really scared me."

He gave her a puzzled look. "You pulled me down on top of you!" She exclaimed.

He was quiet for a while and then said, "Sorry, I didn't realize. Can you help me get up or should I call Gerard?"

"No, I am fine. I will help." She grabbed a towel, dried him off, got him on his feet, and led him to a chair in his closet. "Sit here for a minute, I will grab some clothes for you."

"Shorts in the middle drawer of the dresser, inside the closet." She found a pair of shorts and took it over to him. His skin was ashen, and he had beads of sweat on his forehead. "Maybe I will call Gerard to help me get you into bed."

"I thought you weren't interested." He tried feebly to smile.

This time, she didn't feel threatened at all and smiled right back. "In your dreams, buddy."

Once they got him in bed, she took his vitals. His temp was high, blood pressure was low, and his pulse was racing. She got into his medicine lock box and got out the necessary medications. "Here, take these. Why didn't you tell me you were in pain?"

"How did you know that?" he asked.

"Your vital signs are a pretty good indication. You may also have an infection. Do you want me to call the doctor?"

"No, you didn't give me pain medication, did you?"

"Of course, I did. I am a nurse, it's what I do when my patient is in obvious pain."

"I am an addict. I don't want pain medicine. I have worked too hard to get off that crap."

She softened her stance and sat beside him. "Look, buddy, I get it. I really do, but you know you have a terminal diagnosis, right? You are going to have pain, and unfortunately, it will probably only get worse. I need to treat your pain. It would be inhumane to watch you suffer. Besides, your addiction issues don't really count anymore. That's why you hired me, to monitor and only give you what I think is appropriate. We already had this discussion, remember?"

He quietly scowled. "You need to give me the option."

"Okay, but you also need to trust me. I have been doing this a long time, I know what I am doing. I have dealt with addictions before. I will tell you what meds I am giving you before I give them, does that sound fair?"

"I still don't like it, but I have to admit, I am starting to feel better. Besides, I probably wouldn't know what you are giving me anyway, so I guess I have to trust you."

She monitored his vital signs for the next half-hour. He fell asleep after fifteen minutes, but she stayed in his room for the afternoon. When he awoke several hours later, she was sitting in his chair, reading. He cleared his throat.

"I didn't say anything stupid in my sleep, did I?"

"Not anything I haven't heard before." She smiled. "Feel better?"

"I do. Thank you."

She grabbed her supplies and took another set of vital signs. He grabbed her hand as she reached over to listen to his heart rate. "I'm scared, Claire. I really don't want to die."

She eased his hand off hers and sat back a little. "I know. I can't say I truly understand how you are feeling, but I have worked with the dying for over twenty years. It is scary. And sadly, I can't tell you this is all going to be better. I don't believe in lying or trying to sugarcoat your experience. It doesn't do you any good. I can only tell you that what you are feeling is a normal reaction."

He suddenly became angry. "I don't want it to be a normal reaction. I am fuming!"

"I'm sorry, I wish I could, Brian… but I can't." She turned to walk out of the room.

"Where are you going?" he yelled.

"Just stepping out for a few minutes to stretch my legs and get you something to eat and drink, I'll be right back."

Claire needed a breath of fresh air, and she wanted Brian to have some time alone to process his feelings. She walked through the kitchen to find Marcy and Gerard dancing out on the sun porch. She smiled as she stopped to watch them. Gerard was obviously feeling a little awkward and blushing. Marcy in her wild, wonderful way was teasing him gently and encouraging him. Occasionally, you could see her wince, and her smile was forced as he stepped on her feet a few times and became embarrassed. Gerard looked up from his feet and caught Claire watching them. He jumped back and looked like a little boy who just got his hand caught in the cookie jar.

"Hello… um… Ms. Claire… nothing was going on, I assure you. Marcy was just trying to teach me to dance so I could surprise Sable."

"I didn't think anything different, Gerard. And don't worry, your secret is safe with me. Marcy is a very good teacher," Claire assured him.

"I must get back to work. Thank you, Ms. Marcy for the lesson, and thank you, Ms. Claire. I really want to surprise her."

Marcy laughed. "Go on, Gerry, it's fine. You are improving, only two broken toes today."

His face turned beet red, and he almost ran out of the room. Marcy turned and looked at Claire.

"Good golly, Ms. Molly, thank you for rescuing me. I need to wear padded slippers with that one! What's up, buttercup?"

"Not much really, just needed some fresh air. It's so cute to see you teaching him to dance. Maybe we should give them a date night for him to try out his skills," Claire suggested.

"Great minds think alike sister! I was thinking the same thing. I don't think they have had any time off together in months."

"I'm sure they don't want to leave Brian alone. Speaking of day off, are you planning on going into town anytime soon?"

"I hadn't really thought about it, but it would be fun to hit Duvall Street. Wanna join me? I heard there was a nice little Cuban restaurant we could check out, maybe kick up our own heels and find a hot salsa dancer?"

Claire laughed. "Not for me right now, thank you. I do have a list if any of you go though. I actually might try to get in some paddleboard time in the next few days. Do you think you could sit with Brian for a few hours without drooling all over him or giving him a magazine interview?"

"Maybe, he is pretty hot and gets me all flustered, but I can try and pretend he is my ugly Uncle Gilbert. That might work."

Claire shook her head, grabbed a water out of the fridge, and made a tray to take to Brian. "Is this your famous deviled egg tuna salad?"

"Yes, it is. I am nowhere near as fancy a cook as Sable, but I put it in a tomato and baked it with some mozzarella on top. It was pretty yummy, if I do say so myself."

"Very nice, let's see if Brian approves. It might help your reputation with him." Claire followed Marcy's cue and scooped out a tomato, added the salad in but served it cold with a side of cottage cheese, and added some cold green tea.

She made the same for herself and headed back upstairs. Brian was sitting on the edge of the bed staring at the beach, lost in thought when she walked in.

"Sorry, am I interrupting?" She was struggling with the tray and almost tripped. He stood and walked over, grabbing the tray and setting it on the dresser.

"No, I would actually like the company, if you don't mind."

"Good. You looked like you were a million miles away. Wanna talk about it?"

"How's it going to happen?"

"You mean dying?" She saw the sadness on his face. "It is different with everyone. It's like a journey that is individual to each case. I don't really think you are ready for that yet though, let's talk about something else. One advantage that you have is that you will leave a legacy with your celebrity status. Have you ever thought of writing a book?"

"It's actually funny you should say that. That's the excuse I keep giving the studio about wanting a break to keep them off my back." He relaxed a little and took a bite of food. "This salad is amazing, did Sable make it?"

"Actually, no. Marcy made it. She knows it is one of my favorites. I will tell her you like it. That will make her day."

"Wow, maybe I should give her another shot. She doesn't think I'm a total jerk does she?

"Not at all, she is actually hoping you will forgive her fan club debut. Maybe you should join us downstairs for dinner some night."

"Maybe. I just don't have a lot of energy anymore, but it sounds nice. And I do get lonely sometimes."

"Well, it would be lovely to have you whenever you feel up to it." Claire tidied the room while he ate. She didn't realize she was humming to herself until she looked up, and he was stifling a laugh as he watched her.

"Feel free to laugh if you want, but it won't stop me from singing while I clean. Old habit, I have tried to break it, but that's just me. I can't help it."

"It's lovely, and it makes me smile. I haven't had much to smile about in the last few months. Between watching you singing and listening to Marcy and Sable laughing and joking, I have done a lot of smiling lately. It feels good."

"You've been watching Marcy and Sable?" Claire couldn't help but smile herself.

"I guess I just outed myself, but yes. Gerard and Sable are like my family, and she has been glowing ever since Marcy started helping her. I have become very fond of Marcy actually, but I am still afraid of being with her one on one."

"Oh, you shouldn't. Marcy has been a huge blessing to me for over forty years. She always makes me smile and has stuck by me through a lot of tough times."

"Tell me more about you. You seem to have it all together, is that true or is it a front you put on for everyone else?"

"Sorry, buddy. A long time ago, I learned to set boundaries with patients and that is one of them. This journey that you are on belongs to you, not me. Besides, my life is pretty boring compared to yours, and you look tired. I think I will leave you alone so you can rest."

"I am tired, but you aren't getting out of it that fast. I really would like to learn more about you."

"Maybe another day. I did want to ask you about Gerard and Sable though. I thought it might be nice to let them have a couple days off by themselves since Marcy and I are here. You have other staff here who can help us if we need it. But I overheard Sable tell Marcy, they haven't been able to do anything together in several months. I don't want to overstep my bounds, but I just thought it might be nice."

"Wow, I have been pretty consumed with myself and never realized. Of course, thank you for bringing it to my attention."

"Good. I will take care of it then. I will come back later to check on you but try to rest for now."

Marcy blushed and giggled like a five-year-old when Claire told her Brian loved her salad. Sable and Gerard were thrilled at the prospect of a few days off. Claire got busy booking them for two nights at a local bed and breakfast. She understood that they needed time away, but she knew nothing about running the house and all the jobs Gerard juggled, so she wanted them close if she needed him.

It took Gerard a few days to write out orders and give specifics of what needed to be done. Sable had to leave lists for Marcy regarding meal plans, delivery services, laundry schedules, and housekeeping items that required daily attention. When they were finally ready to leave, Claire looked at the lists and thought she had enough pages to write a book. There were so many things to do with a guideline of how calls were to be handled, passwords for Brian's emails that needed responses, it was all mind-boggling, and she wasn't sure if she and Marcy were up for it. She almost voiced her concerns to Gerard, but when she saw how excited he was to have a few days off, she couldn't do it.

Marcy was a trooper and handled most of Sable's lists. She was also responsible for handling calls and emails from Brian's agent, other celebrity friends, and journalists. She spent two to three hours a day at Brian's bedside, transcribing notes and emails. She always read back what she typed to Brian before sending, and the two seemed to be getting along well.

Claire was responsible for maintaining the compound and keeping staff busy. She became very acquainted with John, the handyman, when not even an hour after Gerard and Sable left, there was a plumbing leak in an upstairs bathroom.

At one point, Claire had logged 47 phone calls and 253 emails that she responded to and that didn't count the number that Marcy had dealt with. Luckily, they had connected with the staff well and met some new faces that Gerard normally dealt with.

Ernesto was the groundskeeper and seemed to have formed a little bit of a crush on Marcy. He followed her everywhere for two days, offering to help lift something or reminiscing of his youth in Cuba. Thankfully Marcy thrived on the attention and showered him back with compliments and questions about the compound's landscaping. Ernesto's assistant, Manuel, was happy to have Ernesto's eagle eyes off of him and on to Marcy. Manuel took over more of Ernesto's chores so that Ernesto was free to help more inside the house.

John was polite and professional but stayed by Claire's side a lot, trying to prove his worth, helping her with as much of the household items as possible. John's wife, Isabelle, stepped in and took over most of the laundry, cooking, and housekeeping. Although she was beautiful and very sweet, she didn't speak a lot of English, making small talk difficult.

All of the staff became very attached to Tank in the short time Claire and Marcy had been there, and Tank was soaking up all of the attention. Claire quickly realized that the entire staff adored Gerard and Sable as much as she did, and they were thrilled at the prospect of helping more. They all helped Claire and Marcy feel a little less stressed and overwhelmed.

She learned a lot about Brian from the other staff members as well. While Gerard and Sable were very secretive about Brian as an employer and his personal life, the others were more than happy to divulge more tidbits. Marcy was an attentive student, telling Claire all the little ins and outs. She had learned that Brian actually had multiple homes at one point all over the world but had sold all but two in the last year. His Los Angeles home was taking a little longer to sell but at one time, he had houses in Milan, Paris, London, and Brazil. He owned condos in the Dominican Republic and Mexico as well. Claire was surprised to learn that he had once owned a home in Haiti and when the earthquake demolished it, he spent several months and millions of dollars helping them rebuild. They learned that most of the animals hanging in the dining room, Brian had hunted and killed himself; but when he became sober, he quit hunting and didn't like to spend much time in the dining room.

Florida was where Brian considered home though; and although he only visited a few times a year before he got sick, this was his largest estate, and it has a very special meaning to him. He mostly came here alone and kept the location secret from his many flings. He did have a few more serious relationships that he would bring for a few days, but this was his personal haven, and he didn't let many know about it.

Claire was also a little embarrassed and humbled to know that Marcy had gotten to know the staff much better than she had in their short time there. She realized working side by side with them like this that she really didn't know much about any of them. She mentioned to Marcy about wanting to get to know them better when Marcy piped up and said, "What do you want to know?"

"I don't know, just a little more of their personal history or stories I guess."

"Well," Marcy began, "Gerard was originally born in England but studied in France and has a master's degree in hospitality management. That's where he met Sable who was going to school as a translator. Did you know she speaks five languages fluently? Anyway they married there, but Sable was raped as a child and couldn't have children of her own, so she didn't really want to get married. She thought about being a nun, but Gerard won her over. Brian met them when he was staying in a hotel that Gerard managed. Brian actually met Sable when he asked Gerard for a translator on a movie he was directing. He didn't realize that they were married, but I guess it didn't make a difference anyway. That's about the time that the building of this compound was nearly complete, and Brian had so much respect for them that he hired them to be the caretakers for the estate. And they have lived here twenty-two years." She stopped to take a breath and continued.

"Now Ernesto was born and raised in Cuba and has a doctorate degree in horticulture. Manuel is actually his nephew but has lived with Ernesto since he was six, and his parents were killed by militia. Pretty cool, huh? Brian met Ernesto in California and actually stole him from that mystery author, Billy Graves. He was at a party there and was so impressed with the landscaping that he had his agent track down Ernesto's name and offered him five times his salary to come work here. Ernesto was more than happy since Graves didn't pay him much and treated him like slime. Manuel is going to Florida State, and Brian helps pay his tuition. Ernesto and Manuel have lived here five years. They have a lot of nice things to say about Brian. But to be honest, I'm not sure Brian pays much attention to them. Ernesto is really good about keeping on the down low and hearing lots of stuff that happens between Brian and Gerard, although he doesn't really gossip. He is just a little nosy. He is very grateful for Brian and being able to be so close to Cuba but stay in the United States."

Marcy thought for a moment and then started again, "Actually when I think about it, I am pretty sure Brian paid for all of them to become US citizens too. John and Isabelle have three children, so they have the largest house in the southeast corner of the estate. John was a real estate developer until the housing crash a few years ago. I know Isabelle was a nanny for some other Hollywood couple, and I think that's how Brian met them. Anyhoo, John has handled the sale of Brian's other homes and has been the contractor fixing up all his homes to sell. They have lived here for about six months, but they have worked for Brian for several years off and on. They just moved around maintaining his other homes for a while. The twins are fifteen, and they have a son who has Down syndrome who is ten. John says that he is Brian's charity case, but he is really loyal to Brian. Isabelle said that John was almost suicidal when the housing crash happened around 2008, and they would have been homeless if it wasn't for Brian. Is that enough, or do you want more?"

Claire stood amazed and humbled. Marcy had taken more time and effort to get to know each of them while she spent all of her time focusing on situations. It was one of the many things that Claire loved about Marcy. Claire was more of an introvert and more detail-oriented, but Marcy loved people. Marcy loved finding out personal things and could get just about anyone to open up to her. Claire hadn't intentionally discriminated, but she realized that she had assumed they were all probably uneducated and undocumented. She made a mental note to herself to practice what she preached about not judging people and realized how she could be thought of as hypocritical.

"Wow, Marcy. Have I ever told you that you are wonderful? And I love you so much for being the kind of person that makes everyone feel special and loved. You are my hero today for telling me these things. I would never be able to talk to people like you do. I admire you so much."

"Well, snickerdoodle, I love you too. Now let's get back to work and not make this weird. His majesty will want dinner soon."

Claire made a point to ask more questions of John while they were working together. She stopped to smile and offer help to Isabelle when she was folding towels. She tried to engage Ernesto, but he only had eyes for Marcy and appeared more annoyed when Claire tried to start a conversation. She realized that work seemed to go much quicker, and the load seemed a lot lighter after getting to know them.

Claire was surprised when she went to deliver Brian his lunch on the third day, and he exploded on her.

"When is Gerard coming back?" he growled.

"Late tomorrow night, why? What's wrong?"

"Why did you tell them they could be gone so long? I only agreed to a day off, not a week! You were not hired to take care of their responsibilities, you were hired as my nurse. You had best keep that in mind. You know nothing about me and how I run my business or my life, is that clear?"

"Crystal clear. But if I don't know what I did wrong, I can't fix it now, can I? And they have only been gone three days, not one week! How could we have screwed up that bad? You have other very capable people here to help care for you. People you have hired, I might add, that are extraordinary at what they do just like Gerard and Sable."

"Just give me my meds and get out of here. I can't deal with all this right now."

Claire went over to get his medication lockbox and noticed bloody tissues in the waste basket. She got his medications and began taking his blood pressure when he jerked his arm away.

"What does all that matter now? I am dying. You are obviously not going to cure me so just give me the drugs, and who cares what my temperature or blood pressure is?"

Claire took a deep breath and tried to shake her defensive attitude. "I still need the information to monitor how much medication you need to keep you comfortable. I may not know how to be a celebrity or run your life, but I do know how to do my job, and you just reminded me that this is what I was hired for." She kept her voice calm and steady.

Brian was obviously not in the mood to discuss it and was fuming. He just glared at her, stuck out his arm and didn't say a word.

Claire decided to leave it alone, handed him his medication and water, and left the tray of food on the bed. She turned to walk away and did not respond when he threw the tray at the wall as she walked out the door.

Claire called Gerard to ask if there was any way they could return early, but it went straight to voice mail. Gerard must have gotten a scathing phone call from Brian because when he returned the call, he simply responded with, "I am twenty miles away and will be there shortly."

Claire chose to stay away from Brian until after Gerard saw him and prayed that Gerard could calm him down. She knew in her mind that all of Brian's actions were part of his grieving process and guessed that he was declining faster than expected. She called the doctor to give him an update and made note of some medication changes he suggested. Marcy burst through the door, frantic. "What's wrong? Why are they back so soon? Where's Brian? Is he okay?"

"Slow down, Marcy. First off, Brian called Gerard and asked him to come back. We must have handled one of his gazillion phone calls wrong, and he is upset. Gerard is up with him now, but I don't have any other answers yet."

Marcy began to pace. "I don't think I screwed up. I went directly off the script Gerard gave me when people called to ask about him. Shoot a pickle! What made me think I could do his job?"

Claire grabbed her by the shoulders. "Look, this is just as much my responsibility too. I don't know what we did wrong, but you have done a great job the last few days, and I couldn't have gotten through it without you so stop belittling yourself."

"Well, Whisper is gonna shoot me if she hears about this. Holy crapola! How do I get myself in these pickles? Do you know what it is like to get scolded by your own kid? Of course you don't, you're perfect."

"Hey there, you know doggone well that's not true. And my kids scold me on a weekly basis, I just choose to ignore them."

Meanwhile Gerard was getting an earful from Brian. Gerard has been in this position many times before and knew exactly how to deal with him. He stood and listened for a good fifteen minutes before he spoke. He had to keep telling himself how sick Brian was and how hard it must be for this man who saw himself as invincible to be in this position. Still it was tough listening to the barrage of cuss words and demeaning tirade without wanting to yell back or punch the guy. Once Brian had calmed down, he simply looked at him and said, "I am sorry you feel that way. What would you like me to do?"

"I don't want you to leave me when I need you most. That's what I want!"

"Won't happen again but just to be clear, you were left with people who truly care about you."

"I know that! But I still don't want them to help me with the same things you do… personal stuff. I don't trust anyone, and I don't want to read in some gossip rag about how I can't control bodily functions. Like it or not, you are the only one I trust. And if you can't deal with it, tell me now."

It took a minute for Gerard to absorb what he had just said, but when the realization of what Brian was dealing with, he understood and truly felt sorry for the guy. He couldn't imagine what it would feel like if he didn't have Sable and was in the same situation. He relaxed his position and assured Brian that he wouldn't leave for more than an afternoon again. Overall this rant was easier to take than when Brian was using drugs; and at least on this subject, he could empathize a lot more. Gerard assured Brian he would be back later in the day to help him with a shower and get the room cleaned up.

"Fine. You are forgiven, now send up Ms. Goody Two-shoes."
Brian snipped.

Claire knocked before entering and walked in slowly. Brian was
very pale and sweaty, there was blood spatters on his pillow. Claire
quietly went to work, taking his vital signs, taking him over to his
chair, and began changing his sheets. She grabbed supplies and
washed his face and hands, helped him brush his teeth and neither of
them spoke. She got a wet washrag and placed it like a neck pillow
around him and as she was pulling her hands away, he grabbed one
and held it close to his face. "Tell me about your God," he said softly.

She was a little startled at first especially since he was so angry
earlier. She took her time and thought about her response. "He has
helped me through so much in my life. I always felt empty before,
nothing ever really gave me peace or happiness. I was always trying to
achieve success… in my marriage, as a mother, my career… nothing
was ever good enough. I kept struggling for something to make me
happy. It wasn't until I began to walk in faith that I ever felt content.
I honestly don't think I would be alive right now if it weren't for God
guiding me through those storms."

"If there is a God though, how come there is so much evil in the
world?" he asked.

"That's easy. God gives us all free will, we can choose to serve
him and allow him to guide us through, or we can choose different paths. We are his children, and sometimes we get ourselves into
predicaments that we need to get ourselves out of. We have to face
consequences so we can learn lessons. Sometimes we have to go down
tough roads to appreciate the good he has waiting for us."

"How can you say that? Do you think children ask for cancer?
Don't good people die in horrific tragedies?"

"First off, a lot of those tragedies are man-made, people like to
place blame on God when we terrorize the earth with pollution and
cause climate change, then expect him to save us when we desecrate
the earth. Secondly those who believe and children have a much better place to go than what they are missing out on here. I don't pretend
to know all the answers. All I can tell you is that we all have choices.
Sometimes evil wins because of choices, either we personally take or

choices our society as a whole take. Faith doesn't take away problems. Faith is there to help you through the tough times."

"I have known a lot of people that believe in God, and he didn't help them at all. They were good people that didn't deserve what they were dealt in life. I look at the suffering in this world and don't know how a benevolent God could stand by and let it happen."

"If people truly believe in God, then they know that this life is temporary, and there is something much greater for them waiting. It does truly hurt me to see so much evil winning, but I have a peace that goes beyond understanding. I am sure the people you know who are believers could tell you the same thing."

"Well, I just know it wouldn't work for me. A lot of the religious people I know are hypocrites. They spout off Bible quotes and then spit on their neighbor. I am a jerk, I know it, accept it, and I don't pretend to be something I am not."

"Unfortunately, none of us are perfect, Brian. We all make mistakes. Being a believer doesn't mean that you won't always make the best choices, it just means that you keep learning and keep leaning on him to give you guidance. I am definitely not perfect. There is only one who walked this earth that was perfect."

"Yeah, well, don't count on me to be a follower of hypocrisy."

"I won't ever give up hope on you, Brian. I pray for you every day."

"I don't deserve or need your prayers, Claire. Just like you said, I got myself here, snd the devil will probably take me out."

"Again free will, Brian. It's your choice, and I agreed not to push it on you. Just know that I am here if you ever want to talk again."

"Thanks for that, Claire. That in itself means more to me than you know."

Claire found Marcy back at the guesthouse packing her clothes. "What are you doing?" she asked.

"I just know he fired us, I have your stuff all ready to go and am almost done with mine," she whined.

"He didn't fire us. He is struggling physically, emotionally, and spiritually. You can't take it personally. He explodes like that sometimes. It's just how he deals with his situation."

"How can you do this all the time, Claire? How can you watch people go through this? I just don't get it. I don't think I am cut out for this. It's not fair."

"I was called to this, Marcy. It's okay if you can't do my job. You were given a different purpose. You bring light, laughter, and love. That's what you do. He could actually use some doses of you and Tank if you're up for it, but I totally understand if you're not. You are free to take Tank home any time. I can always rent a car to get home."

Marcy turned to look at Claire with tears streaming down her face. Claire couldn't remember the last time she had seen Marcy cry which only made her cry too. She didn't realize the toll this job would take on her friend. They hugged and sobbed for ten minutes before Marcy let go and began unpacking the clothes she just put in the suitcase.

"Does this mean you are staying?" Claire asked.

"Of course it does goofball. My crown in heaven has a lot of dents, maybe this will hammer some out."

Claire smiled and dried her eyes.

"Good. How about we both take Tank for his walk tonight. We could both use some fresh air, and I found a path that goes straight to a small beach. Gerard will call if he needs me."

"Sounds like a plan. I still want to go into town soon though. Maybe now that Gerry and Sable are back, I can do that tomorrow. Man I hate crying. There isn't going to be anyone on the path to see my bloodshot eyes and huge Rudolph nose, is there?"

"I doubt it. Most of the day staff has gone home for the night, and I am sure Sable and Gerard are busy unpacking themselves."

"Okay, I'm in. Grab Tank while I blow my honker."

The stroll was just what they needed. For once, Marcy was melancholic, and the beautiful sunset and sea air refreshed them. They sat on the beach, each struggling with their own losses and memories. And as always, they each felt the floodgates of peace and forgiveness wash over them. Both of them jumped when Tank broke their silence and began barking at an iguana on a large rock and began kicking sand everywhere.

"Ah, leave it to Tank, our protector, to get us off our butts and back to the house before it gets too dark to see the path. Atta boy, buddy." Marcy laughed as she distracted him away with a treat.

As they were walking back to the guesthouse, Marcy stopped, took a very deep breath and said, "Okay, kid, I will stay for a little while longer. But when he starts getting really bad, I might have to bolt. I don't know if I can do it, and I still don't know how you do this all the time."

"He doesn't have many real people in his world, Marcy. No matter what he has done in the past, he doesn't deserve to leave this world alone. No one does. Someone has to guide him to the bridge. I know there will be others on the other side, waiting to help him. And I know he has to walk the bridge alone, but someone needs to get him there. I would rather it be a believer who can take him to the right bridge. God called me to do this, and it is an honor to serve him this way."

"Yep, I am never gonna get these dents outta my crown when I have to compete with you." Marcy laughed. "I am gonna end up scrubbing toilets in heaven while you sit at the feast in your mansion."

"Whatever, Marcy. You are going to be the ray of sunshine, and we will all have to wear sunglasses just to look at you."

Brian slept for two days without eating or drinking anything. The four of them took turns sitting with him, placing cool rags on his neck, swabbing out his mouth with water, and placing pillows in various places to keep pressure off different areas. Claire taught them all the basic duties they could all do to help him. Marcy was with him when he finally woke up.

"Hiya, handsome. Did you decide to come back and give us all a hard time again?" she said softly.

"It's what I do best. What time is it? How long have I been asleep?" His voice was scratchy and hoarse.

"Two days which I say, is one heck of a nap. Are you hungry?"

"Starving. Is there any of that salad of yours left?"

Marcy giggled. "Honey, you just made me tickled pink, and I would be delighted to make you some. You want it fancied up or plain-Jane?" Never mind, I will make both. Let me call Claire up, and I will hop right on it."

Claire came in and smiled when she saw him "Welcome back, buddy. How's your pain?"

"Pretty bad, I feel like I can't wake up. Like I am in a fog with knives being thrown at me."

"Well, let's get you something to eat and drink, then maybe a shower. That should make you feel better and might help the fogginess." Claire got him up and helped him into the bathroom. He was weak but able to clean himself a little and brush his teeth. Claire took his vital signs, gave him medicine, and sat him in his chair.

Marcy, Gerard, and Sable all came in carrying something. Marcy with a food tray, Sable with a pitcher of iced tea, and Gerard with a stack of movies and two big bags of popcorn.

"What's all this?" Brian asked.

"A party, sir. You were pretty out of it, and we were all worried. Now that you are awake, we thought some distractions might help. Actually it was Marcy's idea. She thought a movie night was in order. We know you are too weak to go to the theater room, so we just thought we would bring the party to you. Is that okay?"

Brian smiled. "It's great, thanks. Not sure if I will stay awake for all those. Whatcha got?"

Marcy piped up, "Well, I do have your very first movie, *Sandstorm*, which is pretty funny twenty years later, but I thought comedies would best suit the night. Laughter is the best medicine, they say. Here, you're the expert, you pick."

Claire and Sable grabbed pillows from the other bedrooms and made room for everyone to sit. Tank came lopping in the room at the smell of popcorn, slobbering all over himself.

"Who is that?" Brian asked.

"Sorry, that is my fault." Claire blushed. "That's my dog, Tank. I couldn't leave him alone in the guesthouse, and Marcy and I have been staying here the last two nights. I hope it's okay."

"It's more than okay. He's a handsome guy. Come here, Tank." He patted the chair, and Tank sat at his feet the entire time while Brian stroked his head and scratched his hind. Tank was obviously enjoying the attention. They all watched two movies, laughed, threw popcorn at each other which Tank eagerly cleaned up.

Claire kept a close eye on Brian and knew when it was time to wrap up the party. She faked a yawn and stretched. "I don't know about you guys, but I am done for tonight. Gerard, would you mind staying with Brian while he takes a shower? Marcy, how about if you take the dishes down, and Sable and I can change his linens?"

They all got busy, Claire and Gerard got Brian cleaned, changed, and back into bed. Brian settled in and asked if the two could stay for just a little longer. Brian looked at Gerard and said, "I have known you a long time. You have probably been my closest friend. I think of you as a brother. There are some decisions I need to make soon, and I need you to help me. Will you?"

"Of course, sir." Gerard sat down in the chair next to the bed. "What can I help you with?"

"Don't call me sir anymore, Gerard. I just told you I think of you as family. I want you to call Whisper tomorrow and have her send you a copy of my will and power of attorney. Sorry, bro, but you are the only one I trust. Which means you get stuck holding the bag as my executor and power of attorney for both medical and financial. Don't worry though, I have it all very detailed, and the lawyer can help guide you through. Some things have changed in the last few years since I drew it up though, and I will need to make some changes. Can you help me with it?"

"I would be happy to, but are you sure you want me to do that? You have plenty of people who love you and would probably be better equipped to handle such a large estate."

"Like I said, you are the only one I trust. Most people only hang around me for opportunities or for my money. I am sure that after I am gone, there will be plenty of people who say they are family or women who say they had a kid of mine just to get hands on anything their greedy little minds think they can get. I have a couple of legitimate relatives who quit wanting to have anything to do with me once I stopped giving them handouts. They are listed in there, but they get very little. You, Sable, and my other employees will be taken care of, and that is my biggest concern. Claire, are you willing to be a witness when I make the adjustments on the new will?"

"Of course. Did you need anything else from me for the night? I am not sure I am needed in this discussion."

"Not really, but the pain is getting worse. If you could get some medicine before you leave, I think that's all for tonight. Thank you for a lovely evening."

Claire took his vital signs again and gave him pain medication, then quietly left the room as the two finished talking business. She decided that she probably would not need to stay in the main house tonight and fantasized about a nice long swim as she helped Marcy and Sable clean up. Just as she got Tank on the leash and started out the door, Gerard came in and asked if she could talk.

"Can it wait for tomorrow? I was just heading to bed." Claire tried to hide her disappointment.

"I suppose but… I just don't know if I can do this." He began to cry softly.

Claire dropped the leash and wrapped Gerard in a long hug, saying nothing and allowed him to sob softly. Soon Marcy came bouncing in but stopped short when she saw the two. Claire waived a finger no, and Marcy tiptoed out of the room backwards with her hands over her heart, looking as if she might break down too.

"How long does he have, Ms. Claire?"

"Only God knows the timing, Gerard, but I can tell you that if he continues to decline at this rate, it could be sooner than we expected."

He seemed to pull himself together, gave her a weak smile and said, "I didn't realize how much a part of my life he is. I really disliked him for so long, but the fact that he wasn't here much made it bearable. He has only spent weekends or a few weeks at a time here until he got sick. He had several other homes he could have gone to. Why did he choose here?"

"Probably because what he said is true. He thinks of you and Sable as family. You two are wonderful, and I can see why he feels that way. How long have you worked for him?"

"Over twenty years. But as I said, he was rarely here, so it has been a good home for Sable and me. What will we do once he is gone?"

"Pray that God will direct your path, that's all I can tell you. But I have faith you will work it out, and I am sure a compound like this will take a long time to sell. I can't imagine how much someone would have to pay for an estate like this. Maybe the new owner will want help taking care of it as well."

Gerard wiped his eyes and shook his head. "Thank you, Ms. Claire. It has been such a pleasure having you and Ms. Marcy here. I won't keep you any longer. Have a nice evening."

Claire hesitated a few, making sure Gerard had gotten back some composure and would be all right. Marcy knew Claire well enough to know that she needed some personal space so kept to her room and headphones when Claire returned to the guesthouse. Claire swam hard for a good twenty minutes before she allowed herself time to just gently float. She knew from experience that she had to allow herself some time to renew her energies or suffer from caregiver burnout. It had been a very long and intense few days. She thought about asking Brian for a day or two off but decided she would wait a little bit to see how much his condition would change. In the meantime, she thought about his conversation with Gerard. She was overcome with gratefulness, thinking of all the friends and family she had. She had leaned on them so much in the last few years and couldn't imagine what it would be like to have no one.

The next few days were like a dream. Brian was happier, more relaxed, and even came down every evening to join them for meals. He laid out by the pool, did some yoga, laughed, and even joked with some of the staff. Ernesto even came up to Claire and joked if he could have some of the same "feel-good drugs" that she was giving Brian. Gerard and Brian came into the kitchen one night, smiling mischievously and said they had a surprise for them all the next day. They all met in the kitchen at 6:00 a.m. the next morning, and Marcy did not look happy about getting up so early. Her grumpiness soon turned into ecstatic jumping when Brian informed them that he had planned a day trip on the yacht. He gave them orders to gather enough clothes and necessities for the night just in case. Apparently there would be more than just the five of them with the crew. As they boarded, Claire counted seventeen heads when including the three-man crew. Brian had allowed for John and Isabelle's kids to bring some friends to tag along.

Claire got Brian comfortable in the salon and noticed that very quickly, Brian's mood had changed. She almost cringed waiting for an outburst. Without saying a word, she fixed him a tall glass of tea and took his vital signs. Brian grabbed her hand, and she saw he was close to tears. "Tell me, Claire, is it normal to have vivid dreams and hallucinations when you are close to the end?"

"Sometimes, yes. It can be explained with some medications, but I have seen people have discussions with others who have already passed. Did this happen to you?"

"Yes. There are a lot of things I have kept secret for years, and my years of using are very foggy or no memories at all. I had a dream the other night which affected me so much, I decided to do this little trip. I want to see if memories come up so I can try to discern whether it was a dream or a reality."

"Just remember, Brian, that sometimes those dreams are a blend of reality and fantasy. You may get some answers but don't be frustrated if you still can't determine the distinction."

He nodded and found it hard to sit still, so he wandered up to the stern. The crew members were very familiar with the area and found a cove that allowed for them to have some privacy to pull out the paddleboards and small kayak. Claire kept close while paddleboarding and noticed other boats hovering close. She noted one of them would pass by but obviously circled around several times, trying to look inconspicuous, but Claire saw people with cameras. She decided to check on Brian. As she boarded, she found him leaning against the rail with his head down in his hands.

"Hey, Brian, did you notice that boat over there? It has circled around a few times, and I think there are people taking pictures of you. Are you sure you don't want to go back to the salon in case it's paparazzi?"

"I don't care anymore," he said quietly but looked at the boat while heading for the inside.

Claire started to follow, but saw Marcy waving her hands. Claire waved back but saw that she had something in her hand and yelled over. "Did you find buried treasure?" she said jokingly.

Marcy yelled back, "I think I actually did! But not really a treasure, just a few items. I will bring it in."

Claire waited until Marcy took off her gear and came running over. "Look what I found." She was nearly breathless. "This looks like it used to be a shirt before it was fish food. I wonder if someone drowned near here? There is obviously nothing left of a body, but there are some stuff that was kind of buried underneath a rock over in that corner."

Claire looked closely at the jewelry Marcy handed her. It looked like a class ring and a male wedding ring. The wedding ring had some type of engraving, but Claire couldn't make it out. "Go and tell Peter to call the authorities. Maybe they can determine to whom these rings might belong to. It might be as simple as someone lost it scuba diving or snorkeling. Try not to let your imagination run wild, Marcy." Even as Claire said it, she had a sinking feeling that something was definitely wrong.

Marcy went and told Peter, the captain, what she had found. Peter shrugged it off and told her that he would turn it into the authorities later, but he was sure it wasn't anything that required immediate concern. Marcy became frustrated since Peter wouldn't even look at the rings and seemed to blow her off like she was a nagging mosquito.

Marcy found Claire and told her what Peter had said. Brian overheard them and asked what they were talking about. Marcy told him what she had found and saw the color literally drain from Brian's face. He asked to see the rings, and Marcy went to get them from Peter.

While she was headed to the bridge, she saw the boat holding the photographers coming dangerously close and other crew members scrambling and yelling at the approaching vessel. A large bearded man was ignoring the yells and had several cameras strung around his neck which he would juggle while clicking away. In the midst of all the confusion, Marcy tried to recount all the passengers and gather everyone into the salon, but the ship was huge, and there was no way to count every head. She noted that both Gerard and the gardener, Ernesto, were missing as was the kayak. Others were swimming, paddleboarding, or snorkeling on the starboard side. She ran over and yelled at them to board quickly. Meanwhile, Brian's yacht began to accelerate. Marcy was unsure of what to do and was frantic about leaving the area with missing passengers. She ran into the salon to find Brian on the phone, apparently yelling at Peter and covered her ears when air horns went off. Brian slammed down the phone, began cussing loudly when he tried to stand, and became infuriated when he fell back on the sofa.

"Brian, are we in danger?" Marcy asked.

"Peter doesn't think so. He says he just feels it's paparazzi and doesn't think they are armed. However, their boat is much smaller and faster than a 74 ft. vessel, they can potentially get close enough to try and board. The coast guard has been notified and are on the way."

"We can't just leave when we don't have everyone accounted for! Why would he leave the area if he isn't concerned?" Marcy was frantic, and while Claire appeared unconcerned outwardly, she was just as frantic as Marcy inside.

"We can't go far that quickly. And hopefully, the paparazzi will leave when they see the coast guard. I am sure they just are looking for someone famous and don't know who the yacht belongs to. There are plenty of yachts in this area. It has happened before, and Peter knows what he is doing. He will head back to the area when we have protection. Where are those rings you found?"

Marcy stood dumbfounded. "Peter has them, and he is a little busy right now. Why do you care about some stupid rings when we could be in danger? Besides, my old body can't run up and down these stairs like a crazy woman anymore. Can't you just get them when we get this other boat thing settled?"

Brian didn't say anything but turned and went to his stateroom. Marcy just watched and couldn't believe all that was happening. "Has he lost his freaking mind, or has cancer gone to his brain? What is with him?"

"I am sure he has a lot on his mind right now. Something is definitely wrong but leave him alone for a while and let's go up to the bridge to see if we can help."

"Auugghh… who needs a boat this big anyway?" Marcy complained.

As Peter and Brian predicted, the boat carrying the intruders left as soon as they spotted the coast guard boat which arrived about twenty minutes later. Peter was on the radio talking to them and thanking them for showing up so quickly. Once the immediate threat was gone, Peter headed back toward the cove and most of the party were laughing, swimming, and having a grand time. No one seemed very upset that the yacht had taken off without them. Marcy and Claire were surprised when no one even asked if there was a problem as if this were an everyday occurrence.

Jeff, one of the crew members, told the ladies, "This has happened before. We often take different employees out if we are sure Mr. Montgomery won't be returning to the Florida estate for a while. Most of the media outlets and fans know what his yacht looks like and are always trying to get pictures. They get really disgusted when they realize he isn't on board. They will get really close if they think he actually is. Everyone is trained for emergency plans when he does join us."

Instead of being reassured, Marcy became even angrier. "Why didn't anyone fill us in on this before?"

"Sorry, ma'am. We don't often have guests with us that aren't familiar with protocol. I guess we incorrectly assumed Mr. Montgomery would let you know. Besides, we were a little busy dealing with those idiots. They were a little more brazen than most of the jerks we see."

While Marcy and the crew were busy gathering everyone in, Claire decided to investigate her concerns about Brian. She found him in his stateroom lying sideways on the bed. "Can I interrupt for a moment?"

"I suppose. Everyone accounted for? Did they have guns this time?" Brian asked.

"Everyone is accounted for, and how often do they have guns?" She was a little surprised.

"Usually the journalists don't threaten, but I have had my share of crazy fans and stalkers. Those are the ones you can't trust." Brian didn't seem at all fazed by the incident.

"I can't imagine living like that all the time. I don't think I was ever built for the limelight. I am a little curious though about your interest in the rings. Anything special connected to that?"

"Maybe not, but I keep having these dreams and flashbacks. I can't help but think about my past especially when there isn't much to plan for the future. I have this nagging gut feeling that something bad happened on this boat. I can't really determine if it was real or a movie plot I read. I'm just so tired all the time, and I am fed up with feeling like I am in a fog all the time. I sleep, but it doesn't do any good. I feel like I haven't slept in years even after I just wake up. Is that normal?"

"Yes, all of it is normal. The illness itself is what makes you so tired. Your outside body might not feel like you are doing much, but your inside is working very hard to just maintain. The fogginess and dreams may indicate that the cancer has spread. The remembering and life review are a part of your own grieving process. Are you having pain right now?"

"I always have pain, Claire. It is a matter of how much I can tolerate. I don't want any medicine just yet. I really want to think clearly for a little while to see if I can pull this dream apart and find out if it is real or just my crazy imagination."

"Okay, I will leave you to rest. Call me though if you feel like you need something. I don't want you to go too long without pain medication." She slipped quietly away, but she herself had a nagging feeling that she should have pushed him a little more.

Two hours later, they were all exhausted from the day in the water and sun. Claire thought it might be good to head back to the house. Brian still had not emerged from his stateroom, and a few of the crew had over indulged in the alcohol and were getting a little rowdier than Claire was comfortable with. Peter sensed it as well and locked up the remaining liquor. Marcy distracted everyone by putting on some music and turned the lounging area into a dance party. They were amazed when Ernesto grabbed Marcy, and the two began to salsa. Peter stayed in the background and seemed tense. When he headed to the bridge, Claire followed him.

"Is everything okay, Peter?"

"It's fine, ma'am. Go back to the party. We should be docking within the hour," he replied curtly.

"It must be hard staying up here all the time while everyone else is having fun. Oh hey, I forgot to ask you about the rings. Brian wanted to look at them. Do you still have them?"

"Mr. Montgomery does not need to worry about them right now. I will handle it."

Claire wasn't happy about how he kept shrugging her off, and she was worried. Something felt very wrong, but she didn't know Peter well enough to press him. She would talk to Gerard or Brian about it. She turned to leave and felt a chill up her spine when he grabbed her arm, turned her around, and got very close to her. His voice was very soft but firm. "You need to leave this alone, ma'am. There are things about Mr. Montgomery you really don't want to know. Trust me."

He let go of her arm and walked away. She almost ran back into the salon, nearly knocking Jeff over in the walkway.

"Are you okay, miss?" Jeff asked.

"Sorry, I had too much on my mind, I should have been paying closer attention." Claire was still shaken by the encounter with Peter, and Jeff must have sensed it.

"Do you want some water? Are you feeling seasick?" he asked.

"No, no. I am fine, really. Thank you." She headed back to the stateroom.

Brian was standing at his sink, leaning over, and rinsing out his mouth. It was obvious he had been sick. His face was ashen, and his hands were visibly shaking. He turned towards her, his eyes rolled back, and he fell hitting his head on the corner of the marble counter. Blood began pouring from the back of his head. She quickly ran over and grabbed a towel, applying pressure. She screamed for help, but the music was so loud in the lounge—she knew no one would hear her. Brian's cell phone slid out of his pocket, and she found the contact for Peter.

"What now, Brian? I told you, leave it alone!" Peter yelled into the phone.

"Peter? It's Claire. Brian has fallen and is bleeding. Can you or a crew member come help and bring ice?"

She heard him yell at another crew member and hung up on her. Soon there were all three crew members ready to help. His head was still bleeding but slower. She needed her bag so asked the crew to keep the pressure and apply ice. She ran out to grab her bag and had to push past Peter. He grabbed her arm and asked, "Is he okay?"

"Peter, you need to stop grabbing me. I don't like it. Now let me go so I can do my job!" She yelled so loudly at the other crew members stopped and stared at them. His face became red, but he dropped her arm and followed her out.

"I need to know if we can dock or if I need to radio for help. Let *me* do *my* job!" he yelled at her back.

"I won't know until I can assess him better. He will probably need stitches though, so you can call for an ambulance to meet us at the dock."

Peter headed back to the bridge while Claire got her bag and headed back into the stateroom. "Is he always this uptight and unpleasant?" she asked Jeff.

"I have only seen him like this a couple of times before. Usually he is pretty mellow and actually pretty funny. Something has him upset today, that's for sure. Is Mr. Montgomery going to be okay?"

"I don't really know. He isn't responding which doesn't bode well. He has lost a lot of blood." She took his blood pressure and pulse. "Jeff, go ask Peter how long before we dock. We may need to call a Life Flight helicopter."

Jeff pulled out his phone and called. "He can have us there in fifteen to twenty-five minutes, and he already called the ambulance to meet us."

"Well, that will have to do. I don't think a helicopter could get to us sooner. You better go let the others know what has happened so we can clear the way for the paramedics."

A few minutes later, the music stopped. Marcy came running into the stateroom and stopped cold when she saw all the blood. "Holy Toledo! It looks like a war zone in here! Are you bleeding too or did all that come from him?"

"Unfortunately it all came from him. Grab me another cold wet towel please." Marcy stood there just staring while Jeff got the towel.

"Here, Marcy, take this, please." Claire held out the bloody towel. Marcy gagged and ran out. Claire thought about going after her but decided against it and had Luke, the other crew member, go. She could swear she heard her throwing up in the stateroom next door.

They docked soon after, and the ambulance was ready and waiting. Claire rode with Brian to the hospital while Gerard, Sable, and Marcy were going to follow behind as soon as possible. Brian was still unconscious when they arrived at the hospital, and Claire knew from experience the situation did not look promising.

By the time the others arrived, Brian had a CT scan, was stitched up, and lying in ICU. The doctor came in and told them that it was unknown whether he would wake up at all. He verified that cancer had not yet gone to the brain, but Brian definitely had a subdural hematoma from the fall. Marcy, Gerard, and Sable all looked at Claire for translation. Claire explained that Brian had a significant amount of bleeding on the brain, similar to a stroke. Even if he woke up, there may be damage, but it was too early to tell how much. Gerard stood quietly by the bed and took Brian's hand. None of them spoke for a long time. Sable was crying softly, and Marcy was trying to comfort her.

After a while, Gerard turned to leave. The girls all looked at him, questioning. "I can't just sit here. I am going back to the yacht to try and clean up the mess. I will leave the car here and call Ernesto to pick you up if you'd like, or I can come back to get you when you are ready to leave."

"Take the car and Sable," Marcy said. "We can call you when we are ready."

"Actually, let's all go. ICU visiting hours are really supposed to be in fifteen-minute increments anyway," Claire said. "I will leave them our numbers, and they can call if and when there is a change."

"Oh, thank heavens. I am exhausted and staring at these machines is more than I can take right now." Marcy cried as she reached down to give Brian a kiss on the forehead. "Keep fighting, buddy. I still haven't gotten an official autograph, and none of the ladies at my painting class will not believe any of this without it."

Claire stopped at the nurses' station on the way out. They got in the car and realized it was well after midnight, and they were all starving. They found a diner that was still open and stopped. They all got a laugh when the waitress asked what they wanted to drink, and all four said in unison, "Coffee, please."

They each took turns for the next three days at Brian's bedside. Near the end of the third day, Marcy was reading a gossip rag when Brian started twitching. She called the nurse who came and gave him something in his IV. A few minutes later, his eyes began to flutter.

chapter
8

"Well, hiya, good-lookin'." She was holding his hand and smiling at him. He stared at her for a while, but it was obvious he had no idea who she was. "It's Marcy, your favorite pest. Do you remember me?" Brian shook his head no slowly, then nodded and shrugged his shoulders. "That's okay," Marcy cooed. "Although most men never forget me."

The nurse asked Marcy to step out while he performed an assessment. Marcy called Claire and told her to come down. Brian recognized Gerard and Sable immediately. He tried to ask them questions, but it was difficult to focus and form words. He began getting frustrated with himself. Gerard told him a short version of what happened. Brian soon fell asleep, and the nurse advised not to push too hard.

Brian slept off and on for the next two days. And each time he woke up, he remembered a little more. He peppered the four of them with questions at each visit. He began to eat and drink more, and when Claire came in the next day, he was sitting up on the edge of the bed. He smiled at her when she walked in. "You are just the person I wanted to see right now. Go tell the doctor I want to go home."

The nurse that followed Claire in looked at him sternly and said, "I don't think you are ready for that yet, sir."

"I don't give a damn if I am ready. The whole reason I hired her was so that I wouldn't have to die in a miserable place like this." He glared at the ICU nurse. "No offense, but I am dying anyway. So what difference does it make?"

"I'll go call the doctor for you, sir," the ICU nurse stated.

"Well, obviously you are feeling a little better and back to the old Brian of ordering people around."

"That's right. The sooner I get home, the better. I am not paying you a fortune for someone else to do your job."

Claire got defensive and snapped. "Just deduct the days in the hospital from my pay if that's a problem. What is going on, Brian? For a brief moment, I thought you were actually happy to see me."

"I am. Sorry, I need to get home, Claire. I can't have some idiot leak to the press that I am here. I need to get back and talk to some staff. You have to help me, Claire. I am begging you, please!" His tone was urgent and frightened.

Claire looked around to make sure no one was watching. "Calm down, Brian. We told the doctor and nurses here what your real name is, but the rest of the staff thinks you are Jerry Sable. Sorry, it isn't very inventive, but it was what I could come up with quickly. Look at your name band. Besides, you are pretty banged up. I don't really think anyone would recognize you anyway. Take it from me, most hospital workers don't really look at the patients. Plus you are in the ICU, so you're protected from too many people. Please, Brian, calm down and let us do our jobs. I don't think you are ready to go home yet either," Claire begged.

"You don't understand, Claire. The dreams are back, and I need to make some amends. I need to handle some things, and I may need your help. I have to do this before I die, please." Brian looked miserable.

Claire didn't really understand what he was talking about but resigned herself that he was not going to let go of it.

"Let's let the doctor decide. He should be here soon. In the meantime, I will call Gerard and have him get things ready for you."

Four hours later, after arguing with the doctors and nurses, Brian was packed and ready for discharge. The doctor had given Claire strict orders, and Claire had spent the time waiting, calling for various medical equipment like a wheelchair and hospital bed ordered for the house. She called his oncologist to fill him in on the last few days and clarified orders with him as well. Brian slept off and on. And each time he woke up, he became angry that they hadn't left yet.

Claire was surprised when she saw Luke, one of the yacht crew members, was standing in the doorway. He must have sensed her question and quickly stated, "Sorry, ma'am, but Gerard is busy turning the library into a room for Mr. Montgomery. He sent me to pick you two up."

"Remember, Luke, my name isn't Montgomery. It's Jerry Sable, and don't look at me. I didn't come up with that stupid name. Blame her," Brian said sternly, although he was smiling at Claire, so she didn't take offense.

"Right, Mr. Sable. Here I brought you some clothes, sunglasses, and a baseball cap that Gerard sent."

Claire had Luke stand guard at the door while she and a nursing assistant helped get Brian dressed. They were not able to put the ball cap on him with the bandages, but Claire was sure he wouldn't need it anyway. Between the bruising and swelling, he didn't look much like a movie star. They took him out a back exit and loaded him into the car. Claire was worried how they were going to manage since Brian wasn't able to walk and was very weak. It had taken two orderlies, Luke, and Claire to load him into the Jaguar.

Once home, they gingerly unloaded Brian, and Claire got to work, hooking his IVs back up in the makeshift room. She was pleasantly surprised how quickly everything came together, but she supposed it took a large sum of money and a lot of people to put it all in place. Every male staff member was there moving furniture and doing what they could to help. Brian remained awake the whole time, didn't talk much, and only complained of pain during transfers. Once in bed, he seemed to adjust a little more and quickly closed his eyes. Claire took his vitals and was relieved when she noted that he was actually very stable. She gently stroked his forehead and whispered, "May God have mercy on you. I pray you realize it is a miracle you are still here. There must be something very important he wants you to do, Brian. Listen to God and let him guide you."

Brian slept about four hours and was surprised when he woke up and found Claire sleeping in a chair over in the corner with a book on her lap. It took him a few moments to realize where he was and become oriented. Claire must have sensed him and came over to take his blood pressure. He grabbed her hand and held it lightly. "Thank you for being here. You will never know how much it has meant to me."

"You are very welcome. Is there anything I can get for you?"

"The only thing I need right now is to get up and go to the bathroom. Can you help me?"

"You can't really get up just yet. Your legs still aren't strong enough to hold you. You can either use a urinal, or I can place a catheter for you. I wasn't sure which would make you more comfortable."

"A urinal is fine, but I need help sitting up."

She helped him sit up and got everything adjusted for him but realized he was not used to having people watch him urinate, so she busied herself behind his line of view and waited quietly. Once he had finished, she helped him settle back down and readjusted him. While arranging his pillows, he grabbed her hand again. "Can you call Matthew Harper for me? I really need to have a lawyer here and unload some emotional baggage. I would prefer Matthew come himself and not send Whisper, so make sure and tell him that. Will you stay with me though? I don't really want to be alone. I am afraid once I off-load some of these secrets, you won't want to stay, and I really need you."

"Of course. I will have Marcy call Whisper and get Mr. Harper to come down. You needn't worry though, Brian. I am not leaving you. I signed up for as long as you need me."

"You may regret that, but I will take what I can get for now. I'd also like to see Peter. Will you have Gerard call him, please?"

"Of course, let me go find Gerard. Anything else you need for now? You haven't eaten anything since we got home. Anything sound good?" Claire asked.

"Not really, I'm just not hungry, but thank you." Brian lay back and closed his eyes.

Claire left to find Gerard and gave him the message to send for Peter. She found Marcy and Sable in the kitchen making bread which smelled heavenly. Marcy called Whisper who said Mr. Harper was out of the country for the rest of the week but would contact him to see if he could come. Claire decided to take advantage of Brian sleeping and grabbed some things from the guesthouse. She had a strong feeling that she would need to remain in the main house full-time now. She was concerned when she couldn't find Tank. The poor dog must have thought he had been abandoned in the last week. She called Marcy to see if she knew where he was, and Marcy explained that he had already been moved to the main house since Brian didn't seem to mind his presence, and there were plenty of people in and out. She felt relieved but a little jealous. Tank was getting plenty of attention but not from her. She missed the slobbering mutt.

She looked longingly at the pool and decided she could spare a little time. She changed quickly and dove in. She missed her routines. Ever since the day on the yacht, her schedule had been chaotic, and she hadn't had time to think—much less spend quality time alone. Her body needed laps and exercise but her mind needed a break. She closed her eyes and just floated mindlessly for a while. Her thoughts drifted when suddenly, she remembered the rings. "That must be why Brian wants to see Peter," she said to herself and suddenly felt an urgency to get back to the main house. She dried off, skipped the shower, got dressed, and ran back up to find Gerard.

"Did you find Peter yet?" she asked breathlessly.

"Not yet, he isn't answering his phone. The crew members don't work exclusively for Mr. Montgomery however, so he might be working for someone else. I usually have to schedule them months in advance. We were lucky to get them on short notice the other day and very lucky that Luke has been available this last week. Is there a reason for the immediate request?" Gerard looked perplexed.

"Is Luke still around? I'd like to go down to the yacht to look for something." Claire evaded telling him the whole truth. She was afraid she might sound crazy; she didn't have a reason for concern, but something was nagging at her.

"I think he is still on the grounds. I will call him. Did you lose something, Claire? It's not like you to be so..."

"*Insane* is the word I think you are looking for, Gerard. And no, it isn't like me. I leave hysterical to Marcy, but I can't shake the feeling that I really need to get to the boat."

"Let me wrap up a couple of things here, and we can go down to the dock together." Gerard could sense that Claire was not letting go of this feeling or whatever it was she was experiencing, and his own curiosity was sparked.

Claire peeked in to check on Brian and found him still sleeping but very restless. He was mumbling incoherently and flinging his arms. She stroked his forehead, adjusted the sheets, and he calmed down. She put some soft music on and asked Marcy to sit with him. The last thing she needed was to get Marcy involved quite yet, she didn't need two crazy ladies looking for trouble if it wasn't there.

By the time they reached the dock, the sun had begun to set, and Claire stopped midstride at the sheer beauty. The sun appeared to set the ocean on fire with a brilliance that always took her breath away. She marveled at the clouds and took in a deep breath. Gerard had been walking slightly ahead and when he turned to say something, he noticed that she was farther back. He allowed her a moment and realized how often he took for granted just how magnificent his view was. Claire slowed her stride and pointed to some clouds when she caught up with him. "Look, Gerard, there is a cross in the cloud breaks. God never ceases to amaze me with constant signals that he is with us."

"I'm ashamed to admit that I was just thinking of how much I take this beauty for granted."

They walked a little slower with less urgency. The sound of the waves and gentle breeze surrounded them both with a sense of peace. Unfortunately that feeling of serenity would not last long. They entered the salon, and Gerard noted that no one had been in to clean up and became angry. They walked into Brian's stateroom and found blood caked into the carpeting and spattered all over the walls.

"This is disgusting! Part of the agreement with the crew is that they make arrangements to have the boat cleaned whenever they take it out. I don't know how we are getting those stains out now!" Gerard fumed. Claire was taken aback slightly as she had never seen Gerard angry. She had to admit, if she were employing the crew, she would be just as upset.

She turned to walk out and noticed an envelope on the bedside table addressed to Brian. It was bulky and had "PRIVATE" in bold red letters. She picked it up and handed it to Gerard. "I didn't notice this the other day, but then again, we were a little busy in here. Do you know how old this is?"

He picked it up and shook his head. "I suppose we should deliver it to Mr. Montgomery, though. He would know if it was in here before. Do you know what you are looking for? I'd like to get back and make some calls to get this place cleaned up before Mr. Montgomery wants to use it again."

"Honestly, Gerard, I don't know what I am looking for. I just have a terrible feeling in my gut every time I think of this boat. I prayed for guidance before we came down here, but I really just don't know. Can we check the bridge just for peace of mind?"

"Certainly, I never argue against a woman's intuition."

They did a quick run through of not only the bridge, but every room. Claire shrugged her shoulders and decided it must be a post-menopause freak impulse. "Let's go back, I am so sorry to drag you down here. But good news is, we know we need to make calls to get this mess cleaned up."

"Agreed. I have a sinking feeling that Mr. Montgomery's stateroom will need a complete overhaul to get all that blood out."

When they got back to the main house, Gerard handed Claire the envelope and asked her to deliver it. She went into the library and found Marcy reading to Brian while he drank a green concoction she had made. The look on his face was priceless when he saw Claire and held up the glass. His face was almost as green as the smoothie. Marcy lifted the bottom of the glass and joked, "Drink up, Monty, it's good for you. Trust me."

He took a tiny sip and choked. "How can something so horrid be good for you? Sorry, Marcy, but this is disgusting. I will pay you $1,000 right here and now for you to finish it."

"Done deal." Marcy grabbed the glass and chugged it down in four swallows. Her entire upper body wiggled and shook then she smacked her lips. "Aah… hand over the bucks, buddy. And don't think for one minute you are getting out of drinking it. I am going to make another one, but this time, I may add some organic honey to make it a little easier going down."

Claire laughed. "Sorry, Brian, but I gotta tell you, her smoothies do work. I've had to choke down many over the years, but they certainly kill what ails ya."

Marcy left with a promise to return shortly. Claire took her chair at his bedside and handed him the envelope. "Gerard and I went down to the yacht to look for something and found this in your stateroom. Did you leave it there?"

"I have never seen it before. Who is it from?" He took the envelope and examined it closely.

"No clue, but it was on your bedside table. I didn't remember seeing it there before, but I didn't really pay attention either. We were all a little busy that day."

"Well, let's open it and see then." He tore off the tape across the top and looked inside. A flash drive fell out when he pulled out some papers and a photo. His face went completely ashen when he saw the picture.

"What is it? What's wrong?" Claire started to grab the envelope, but Brian yanked it back. He looked at her and with an eerie calm said, "Call Harper now. I don't care where he is, I want him here now."

"Okay, I'll go tell Marcy."

"Not Marcy! You call him. I know you can reach him. He was your lawyer too. Get him now and leave me alone for a while."

"Brian, I don't think I should leave you alone right now."

"I need time alone, and I need my phone. I am trying to be nice, but if you are still here in three seconds, I won't be. And you can't guarantee my language is clean once I get on this phone."

Claire was in no mood to listen to him scream at her, so she handed him his cell phone and left quickly. She was nearly in tears when she closed the door behind her and dialed the lawyer's office. She did start to cry when she heard the message on the end of the line saying the office was closed. She had no choice but to have Marcy call

Whisper. Marcy tried to stay calm, but she could tell there was something wrong when Claire asked to see her phone. Claire just simply shook her head no when she grabbed the phone and stepped out of the room. She called Whisper and again got a voice mail. She asked Whisper to call her back as soon as possible and left her cell number.

When she handed the phone back to Marcy, she couldn't look her in the eyes or she knew she would just break down and full-out cry. She needed to collect her thoughts. She found Tank in the kitchen under Sable's feet, waiting patiently for her to drop food off the counter. She grabbed the leash and he reluctantly followed her outside. They walked down the path to the beach and as soon as she stopped, Tank flopped down in the sand and rolled over to get his belly rubbed. That was all it took. Claire began to cry and laugh at the same time. She rubbed his belly for a few minutes, then laid her head down on him. He sensed she needed him, flipped over, and licked her face. They sat there cuddling for a little while until he saw a rabbit and then he was off. She didn't run after him since she knew he would be back fairly quickly since he never ran far or for long. She sat looking out at the waves and was tempted to jump in and take a swim. She was lost in her own little world and didn't pay much attention when she heard rustling behind her. She called Tank over and nearly screamed when she heard the reply, "I don't take orders, lady."

She turned and saw Peter standing behind her. "Get up," he said.

"Peter, what are you doing here?"

"I said *get up!*"

Claire scrambled to get up and tried to assess her danger level. "Peter, I'm up. What is wrong?"

"You know what's wrong, you saw the envelope. I watched you take it from the yacht."

"I didn't look inside. I swear, so I really don't know what you are talking about."

"You are such a liar. You and your weird friend are very nosy and like to get into everyone's business where you don't belong. You don't belong here."

"Look, Peter, I am a nurse. I am here for Brian and not to get into anyone's business. Trust me, I hate confrontation. I am not looking to get into any trouble with anyone."

"Why does Brian need a nurse?"

"He's... wait, you don't know?"

"No, he never said he was sick, so why does he need a nurse?"

"Why don't you ask him? He wants to see you. He's been trying to call you."

Peter pulled out a gun and pointed it at her. "Yeah, and you know why. Don't lie to me. I have had enough lies!"

Claire held her hands up and started inching backwards. "Please, don't hurt me. I will tell you, I promise. Just put the gun away please," she begged. She didn't see Tank, but she heard his low growl, and before she could say another word, he came, teeth baring and barking, and jumped on Peter. He knocked the gun out of Peter's hand which discharged, and Tank went for Peter's throat. Claire didn't know what to do but run.

She ran back up toward the house, screaming for help. Ernesto and Manuel ran up to the clearing and asked what was wrong. Claire pointed down the path and breathlessly said, "Tank... Peter... help me." They took off down the path and appeared a few minutes later, carrying a bleeding Tank.

"Oh Lord, what happened to him?" she cried. His leg was bleeding, and when she went to pet his head, he whelped.

"I don't know, but let's get him to a vet soon," Ernesto said.

"What happened back there?" Manuel asked.

"Peter... he had a gun. I don't really know what he wanted. He seemed to think I had information that I don't have. Did you see Peter down there?"

"No," Ernesto replied, "all we saw was your dog laying there, bleeding."

"Okay, put him in Marcy's car. I will grab the keys."

She sprinted into the house and asked Marcy for the keys. "They are in my purse down at the guesthouse. What is wrong with you? You've been weird and secretive the last two days."

"Marcy, I need the keys. Please come with me to get them. Tank was shot, and I have to take him to the vet."

"Whaaattt? Why didn't you say so, sugarplum? Let's go, I will drive. You hold Tank."

Claire really didn't want Marcy to come but decided she was too freaked out and shaking, so it was probably a good idea to have someone else with her. They each grabbed their purses and headed to the car. Poor Manuel was getting tired from carrying 87 lbs. of dead weight. Tank was breathing hard, tongue hanging out, and whining. Claire got in first and had Manuel lay him on her lap in the back seat. Ernesto had thought to grab a rag and wrap it around Tank's flank where he was bleeding. As they pulled out of the driveway, they both realized they had no idea where they were going. Claire asked for Marcy's phone and got directions to the nearest emergency vet clinic. She passed Marcy's phone up to her then called Gerard on her phone. "Gerard, call the police. Peter had a gun, threatened to shoot me, and shot Tank. We are on the way to the vet clinic right now. I will call you once we get there and get him seen."

Marcy slammed on the brakes when she heard Claire's conversation. "What in the Sam Hill happened back there? Peter tried to shoot you? I thought Tank got hurt on a rock or something!"

"Marcy, please. I will tell you all of it later, can we please just get Tank help right now?"

"Oh merciful heavens, of course." She turned around and drove quickly, blowing through every stop sign on the way. Luckily they didn't have much traffic, and they avoided Duvall street.

"Slow down, Marcy. You are going to get all of us in the emergency room if you aren't careful, not to mention a ticket," Claire warned. Her adrenaline was already pumping at full stream, and she couldn't stop shaking. Tank laid in her lap, whining softly and licking her leg.

Marcy pulled into the parking lot and yelled back, "Wait here, I'll get help."

Claire waited, stroking Tank's head and crying softly into his neck. "I am so sorry, buddy. Thank you for saving me. You are my hero."

Two assistants came out and helped Claire and Marcy get him out of the car. Thankfully Marcy took the lead and gave the receptionist all of the information while Claire went back into the exam room. The staff was very efficient and had him on an IV and cleaning the wound within minutes.

"We are probably going to need X-rays to see if he has any damage, but it looks like it is a superficial wound on his flank. Can you tell me what happened?"

Claire gave a brief description of events and then repeated it to the doctor when she came in. "I think we ought to keep him overnight for observation, and I would like to stitch his flank. He is crying pretty hard when I palpate his neck. I would like to run some tests if that's okay with you."

The doctor had a very calming effect on Claire, for which she was very thankful. "That's fine doctor, whatever you feel is best."

"Good," the doctor said as she began to write out orders. "Leave your information at the front desk, and we will call you with updates. I don't really suspect much damage, but I would rather be safe." She looked over at Claire and smiled, "Maybe you should get checked out too. Sounds like you have really been through a lot today. Don't worry about Tank, we will take good care of him and call you tomorrow."

Marcy was pacing in the waiting room, biting her nails when Claire emerged tearful and without Tank. "Oh my stars," Marcy cried. "Is he dead?"

Claire shook her head no, smiled, and hugged her friend.

"No, Marcy. He is probably just fine. It was just a laceration on his flank, but they want to run some tests, so they are keeping him overnight. They don't really feel like it is serious."

"Oh, thank you, baby Jesus!" Marcy sang. "You can't tell me the Lord doesn't love that adorable drooling bulldog as much as we do!"

"I agree, let's get back to the compound as soon as possible. I am sure the police are there by now." Claire paid a deposit to the vet and tried to brush off as much of Tank's hair off her pants as possible.

While driving back, Claire received a call from Brian demanding to know why the police were at his house and what happened. She gave him a brief rundown of her encounter with Peter. He begged her not to say anything to anyone about the envelope until his lawyer arrived and hung up before she could argue. Claire was so distraught. How was she supposed to keep the envelope out of her report? That was the whole reason Peter threatened her!

"What envelope did Peter want? I knew that guy was crooked with the way he acted about the rings on the boat!"

"That must be it, Marcy! You are brilliant! Of course! Why didn't I put it together sooner?"

"Wait, what? What did I put together? If I am so brilliant, why do I not have a clue as to what you are talking about?"

"It's the rings! There has to be something going on with those rings! Do you know if Whisper got in touch with Matthew Harper? Brian won't tell me anything until he is here." Claire couldn't remember if she had actually gotten in touch with either of them.

"All I know is that Harper won't be back in the country until day after tomorrow. Now what is all this about? What have I missed?"

"I can't really tell you much because there are too many things I don't know myself, and Brian won't fill in the blanks until Harper shows. You really do know as much as I do at this point. I just have to figure out what I am going to say to the police if I can't talk about the envelope."

"See... I don't know! What about the envelope?"

"Gerard and I found an envelope addressed to Brian on the yacht earlier today. When Brian opened it, he freaked out and said he needed Harper right away and wouldn't say anything about the envelope contents until Harper got here. I know there was a photo and a flash drive in it, but that's all I know. I am only guessing that the rings have something to do with all this."

"Oooohhh... must be Peter trying to blackmail Brian, but for what? I still don't understand what the rings have to do with it."

"I don't know... maybe that's why I am a nurse, not a detective. It sounded right in my head but when you say it out loud, it really doesn't correlate with the envelope, otherwise the rings would probably have been in the envelope, right?"

"Honeybunch, this whole story has me boggled, so don't ask me if any of it makes sense."

When they arrived, there were two police cars parked outside the main house. Claire and Marcy found Gerard speaking with them in the front great room, and all three stood when the ladies arrived.

"Mrs. Roberts?" The first one shoved a pudgy little hand toward her which she reluctantly shook.

"Yes, I am Claire Roberts, and this is my friend, Marcy Sinclair." Pudgy-cop held out his hand for Marcy.

"Pleasure to meet you both. May I speak to you in private, Mrs. Roberts?"

"Of course, but everyone here knows the story, and I don't mind if they are present." Claire was hesitant not knowing what Brian wanted her to reveal just yet. She didn't want to put anyone in danger, but she also knew she couldn't lie.

"That's fine then. Can you tell me what happened earlier?" Pudgy asked.

"All I can tell you is that Peter came behind me and scared me. He asked what Marcy and I were doing down here and how we are related to Brian. He pulled a gun out, and my dog interceded on my behalf, allowing me time to run. I heard a shot, took off running toward the clearing and found the groundskeeper who helped me get my dog to the car, and we left for the emergency vet clinic. I called Gerard to alert him of what happened and to call you."

"Do you have any idea why he would pull a gun? Why was he so interested in your relationship with Mr. Montgomery? What exactly is your relationship with Mr. Montgomery?" Pudgy looked at her as if she were lying or hiding something. Claire really did not feel comfortable being interrogated.

Marcy spoke up. "We are friends of family and have been visiting for the last month or so."

Claire felt Marcy's support and added, "I really have no idea what Peter wanted. I'm sorry I can't help more, it all happened so fast and then I was so worried about my dog…"

Pudgy was obviously not happy with the story but shrugged his shoulders, stuffed his little notebook into his jacket, and turned to Gerard. "We will put a lookout for Peter. Do you want me to post a guard?"

"I don't think that is necessary, Jim. Thank you for your time. I will call you if we need anything else," Gerard answered.

"Okay, well, let me know when we can speak with Mr. Montgomery." He turned and spoke with Claire and Marcy. "Ladies, please stay close to the compound and call us if we can be of further service. Here is my card." He gave them each a business card, tipped his hat to Gerard and left. The other officer nodded and smiled at each of them as he followed Officer Pudgy out the door.

Once gone, Gerard looked at Claire with a sigh of relief and gave her a hug. "I am so glad you are okay Claire. Thank you for protecting Brian. I don't really know what's going on, but I intend to find out. How is Tank?"

"I think he will be fine, but they are keeping him overnight to run some tests," Claire said as they headed into the library. Brian was sleeping but woke up as soon as the heavy door closed. He looked up and smiled when he saw Claire.

"I am so glad you are okay. I only got bits and pieces of the story. What happened?" He sat up a little straighter and grabbed her hand.

Claire recanted the whole story this time; and when she finished, she looked at Brian, gathering some strength.

"After all that, I feel like I deserve to know what is going on. I didn't tell the police the whole story which makes me very uncomfortable, but I am trying to protect you as well. I have a feeling that the envelope is connected to all this. Is Peter blackmailing you?" She pulled the chair over to the bed and sat facing him.

"Yes, he is. And yes, you deserve to know the truth. You all do. I never imagined that any of you would be in danger, but I honestly need to have Harper here when I tell the whole story. Can you be patient for one more day? I talked to him about an hour ago, and he is flying in tomorrow. I need to clear my conscious and have it on tape. I need to tell him the story first and have him decide how to proceed. Is that fair enough?"

"I guess it will have to be since I don't seem to have much of a choice in the matter." Claire sighed.

"In the meantime, I think it is a good idea for both of you to stay in the main house tonight," Gerard interjected. "I will let Ms. Marcy know. Is there anything you need from the guesthouse, Ms. Claire?"

"No, Gerard, I already have most of my things here. Thank you." Claire went to the lockbox to give Brian his medications. She was concerned about all the stress and how it would affect him physically. She handed him medication and realized he was still connected to the IVs. She made a quick decision that he was stable enough and began disconnecting the tubing. Brian noticed that her hands were visibly shaking hard.

"Claire, sit down. You have been through a lot today. I am okay, I promise. Tell me what's wrong."

"Are you kidding me? My dog was shot today, I had a gun pointed at my face. I am trying to be patient, but I don't know what is happening. And right now, I just want to go home, but I know I can't. That's what's wrong."

"You can leave whenever you want. I am sorry you got dragged into all this, that was never my intention."

"Ugghh, I know, Brian. But honestly, I have a bad gut feeling. I haven't had this gnawing in my gut since my husband died, and I am not sure I can handle another situation like that one."

"I am truly sorry, Claire. Can you tell me about him? All I know is what I read in the papers, it was a pretty hot story. But I also know you can't trust everything you read."

"He was good to me. He was an introvert which was so different from me. Before we met, I was a lot different than I am now. Partly because I was young and wild. I used to be the life of the party, always had people surrounding me. He gave me a peace and tranquility that I desperately needed but didn't realize it. Does that make sense?"

He nodded his head and just listened, she smiled remembering, "He was totally the opposite of me. I was a single mother at the time, and he never really wanted children, so our beginning was a little shaky. Over the years though, he became a little more outgoing, and I became more comfortable with being alone, less needy, I guess. He always supported me with whatever I wanted to do, he loved me for who I was and never asked me to change myself in any way. But looking back, we both changed a lot, and we grew together. That doesn't happen very often. We were lucky." She looked at her hands that were still shaking. Tears began falling, but she kept her voice strong. She just couldn't look at Brian. She toyed with her wedding ring. "I remember him being upset with me for getting involved in situations when I really should have kept my nose out of it. I guess that was why it was so hard to fathom his death. Normally he would never step in like that. He never wanted to be a hero. He liked staying back and letting others who knew what they were doing take charge."

"Maybe you rubbed off on him more that he wanted to admit."

"Maybe. Anyway, I will never know what made him investigate his boss like that. He never talked about his work and neither did I. I couldn't talk about my work at home. And whenever I would ask him about his, he was vague and only provided little bits of his day. Although I know he was proud to be working at the Veteran's Hospital and maybe that's what spurred him to do something so unusual. But when he found out the owner of the construction company was skimming off the government bid and supplying cheap materials for a premium cost, he began taking pictures of invoices on his phone, then taking pictures of the products they were using which were of far less quality. When I got the call that he had fallen, I knew something was very wrong. My husband was a perfectionist at everything he did and safety of his crew always came first. Then I found his phone and texts he would send from his work phone to his personal phone, and things started coming together. Marcy and Whisper advised me to get a lawyer before I went to the police and well… the rest is history. The story went national, and so did his case. I will never know who recorded his murder and although it was horrendous to watch, I am thankful that he/she turned it in when they did. Police won't give me any information and said whoever it is solved the case and is now in protective custody. Dirk hated the spotlight though and would have been horrified if he were alive."

She stopped, realizing she hadn't talked to many people about Dirk and never to a patient before. "I'm sorry, Brian, I shouldn't have poured out my sob story to you. Peter must have frightened me more than I realized. This whole experience has brought up a lot of feelings I should not be sharing with you. You have enough to deal with."

"Please don't be sorry. I am honored to hear some of his story. If I were well enough, I would probably make it into a movie. I have to tell you, though, you may be very uncomfortable with the things I need to talk to Harper about. I understand if you can't handle it and need to leave. All this business with Peter has added to my suspicions about something that happened several years ago on the boat. I have been having very vivid dreams about an incident, and I need to find out for sure what happened. The hardest part of this story is that I don't remember. Peter is blackmailing me, but his version of the story is not adding up with my dreams. I don't know which to believe. I am sorry, I do trust you, but that is all I can say for now."

"How about if we just take one day at a time? I honestly can't think about much more right now." Claire honestly didn't want to make promises to stay if she or Marcy were in any real danger, but she would have to have faith that God would tell her when to leave.

"Deal. But I do need to ask you not to mention what I just told you to anyone. At least not for now. Let me talk to Harper tomorrow and show him what Peter is blackmailing me with and decide where to take it from there."

"I can do that. Unfortunately, I am pretty good at keeping secrets."

Both Claire and Brian were exhausted. Claire finished her nursing duties and told Brian she was going to bed. She hadn't had dinner, but she really wasn't hungry. She really wanted to go for a swim but wasn't sure she was up for it. Brian was asleep before she left. She was worried about him too. He was sleeping so much more, not eating, had more pain, and having more dreams. She wondered how much of his dreams were memories and how much was simply a result of his subdural hematoma. She was amazed at how well he was doing and knew that it wasn't normal for someone to be so alert and cognitive after all his body had been through.

She opted for a nice hot shower over a swim and settled in to read some mail that Maria had sent to her. Most of her bills were on automatic payments, but there were still a few she needed to deal with. She was pleasantly surprised to see some photos of her grand-children and wished she could be with them right now. They were growing so fast, and she rarely went this long without seeing them. FaceTime and Skype were great but not the same. She made a prom-ise to herself when she moved from Colorado to Florida that she would travel back or send them out as often as possible. They would be out of school soon, and she was missing out on her summer plans. She sent an email to all three of her daughters, asking if they wanted to come for a visit. Whisper would just have to find someone to cover for her for a few days. She felt lonely for the first time in a long time, missing her husband terribly. When she finally crawled into bed, she grabbed the pillow on the empty side of the bed, buried herself into it, and cried herself to sleep.

Matthew Harper arrived around nine o'clock the next morning looking very haggard and jet lagged. Marcy fawned over him, fixing him breakfast, and telling him all about the last month. Matthew was a ruggedly handsome man in his late thirties; and although he was a lawyer, he was a man of few words. Marcy was always trying to get Whisper and Matthew together in more than a working relationship and would have loved to have Matthew as a son-in-law. Matthew quietly sat, listening to Marcy ramble, nodding every so often to assure her that he was listening. Claire and Gerard were in the library trying to rouse Brian and get him ready for an interview, but he was only minimally responding. Claire was hesitant to give him his morning medication, she needed him alert and cognitive when he talked to Mr. Harper.

Matthew was patient and took advantage of the time to jump in the shower, catch up on his messages and emails while Brian was sleeping. He had never been to the Florida compound before, and Marcy was all too eager to show him around. After lunch though, he pulled Claire aside and asked if she expected Brian to wake up soon. He had interrupted other clients to rush down here and was afraid it might have been a waste of time.

Claire called Gerard down, and they took Harper into the library. Claire gave him the envelope, the flash drive. She told him the events with Peter and what Brian had told her about Peter blackmailing him. Neither Claire or Gerard had looked in the envelope and were hesitant to hand it over, but they weren't sure what else to do. Harper asked Gerard to fetch his computer and went to Brian's desk to inspect the contents of the envelope. It took everything Claire had in her not to stand behind Harper as he was scanning them. Instead she went to Brian's bedside and tried to arouse him. Harper showed no emotion the entire time but would frequently look toward Brian to see if Claire was successful.

When Gerard came back, Matthew loaded the flash drive and noted it was a video. He watched but put headphones on so neither Claire or Gerard could hear the contents. After an excruciating fifteen minutes, Claire couldn't stand the suspense any longer. She gave Brian a sternal rub, and he fluttered his eyes. "Brian, Harper is here and has been all morning. He is going to leave if you don't wake up. Please open your eyes," she begged.

He mumbled, "Don't believe it. I didn't do it and can prove it."

Harper came to his bedside. "Brian, it's Matt. Hey, how can you prove it?"

"I... drugged... dreams..." Brian slurred, then closed his eyes again.

"Okay, buddy, I will handle it," Harper assured him. He turned and motioned for Gerard to follow him. Claire started to follow as well, but Matthew held his hand up. "Not yet, Claire. I will try to get answers for you soon, but I need to speak to Gerard alone first."

They went to Gerard's quarters so as not to be overheard. "Okay, Gerard, I am going to give you the basics. Peter is blackmailing Brian. He states that Brian killed a reporter on the yacht about a year ago and has proof. He says that Brian has been paying him off to keep quiet but doesn't want to go to jail, and the money isn't enough for him to stay quiet. Do you know anything about any of this story?"

"No, sir, I don't. I'm sorry. I can tell you that when we were on the boat, Marcy found some rings diving, and Peter's entire demeanor changed after that. Maybe you should ask her what she found."

"I am having difficulty as an officer of the law not to report this. I really need to hear Brian's side of the story and get more information before I turn it over to the authorities though. I am going to make some phone calls and hire a private investigator. I can't stay here much longer, maybe a day or two. But then I really need to get back to an ongoing case in London. I don't expect that one to wrap up for another week, and the longer I am gone, the tougher it gets to clear my schedule."

"I understand, let me go see what I can find out from Marcy without stirring up her curiosity even more. Feel free to use my private office, you can lock the door. I will notify you if Mr. Montgomery wakes up." Gerard showed him where the office was and gave him the key.

"Thank you, Gerard. I need about an hour, and then we can all gather in the library, and I will update you all with what I can."

Marcy and Sable were in the kitchen making pies when Gerard came in. "Sable, darling, would you call the vets office and inquire about Tank please? I am sure Claire would like to have him back as soon as possible."

Sable took the hint and went into another room to call. When Gerard and Marcy were alone, he looked at Marcy and shrugged his shoulders. "Mr. Montgomery still hasn't awakened, and Mr. Harper is being very secretive about all this. I just wish we could figure out the link to this mystery. Nothing has been the same since that day on the boat. Unfortunately, I was enjoying my time in the water too much to know what really happened."

"Don't ask me, Gerry. I am as confused as you are. I am sure that jerk Peter is off in the wind now too. To top it all off, the little twerp never gave me back the rings I found that day."

"What rings, Marcy?

"I was diving near the cove and found a wedding band and a class ring with some scraps of what must have been a piece of clothing under a boulder near the waterfall. I gave them to Peter to turn into the coast guard, but then he got busy with that boat of photographers. He was a real jerk when I asked him about it later. I really hope he turned them in when the coast guard was there. After all that excitement, I had a little too much wine and dancing, so I forgot about it. Then of course Brian fell, and the rest is history, so they say.

After Claire's run-in with him, I don't think I am too anxious to hunt Peter down to ask him about it now."

"Interesting, do you remember what they looked like? I could call the coast guard and see if Peter turned them in."

"Oh, that's a great idea. Maybe they can send over a handsome sketch artist, do you think the coast guard has those or only the police?"

Gerard chuckled. "I'm not sure but I will make sure to ask just for you. Although I am not sure, I will specify to send a cute one if they have it."

"Oh, Gerard, you are no fun. Hey, do you think Monty is going to pull out of this? He is sleeping all the time now, and he looks horrible, but don't tell him I said that. He really has lost weight and looks like a skeleton now instead of the Greek God bod he had just a few weeks ago."

"You'll have to ask Ms. Claire about that, but you are right. He does not look well. I wish there was something I could do for him. Maybe figuring out this whole Peter mystery will help boost his spirits. I know the stress of all this surely can't be helping."

Marcy and Gerard were standing close to each other with their voices down and neither one heard Harper come into the room. He was standing behind Marcy when she turned around and ran directly into him. She yelped loudly and slapped him on the arm. "Heavens have mercy! You scared the dickens outta me, Matthew Paul Harper! Don't you know that you should never scare old ladies? I about peed my pants, and I don't wear Depends!"

"Marcy, no one calls me by my middle name except my mother. How do you even know it? Never mind, I don't want to know. Gerard, Brian is awake and mumbling something. I wonder if you could come in with me?"

Marcy chimed in, "I will make him one of my smoothies and bring it in for him."

Harper turned and held up his hand. "Can you give us some privacy for a few moments, please? I will let you know when you can come in. Thank you, Marcy. And I am sorry for frightening you."

Marcy huffed. "I wasn't gonna eavesdrop, Matthew. And just so you know, I already know a lot more than you think I do, Mr. Smarty-pants. Don't make me call your mamma."

Harper had to smile. "Marcy, I appreciate all you have done here. I have gotten glowing reports about how helpful you have been. There are just some questions I need to ask in private. I will keep you updated, I promise."

"Okay, fine, but I am still making him a smoothie." Marcy turned as Sable came back in, and Claire followed soon after. "Good timing, Ms. Claire," Sable said. "I just called the vet's office to get an update on Tank. They said he is ready for pick up anytime. They were giving him a grooming session but said they should be done before you get there."

"Oh, thank you, Sable! I hate to admit it, but I haven't thought to call all morning. Since Mr. Harper and Gerard are having a confidential meeting, maybe they wouldn't mind if I slipped out to pick him up."

Sable volunteered to go with her while Marcy fixed smoothies. Sable was normally very quiet but spoke up once they got into the car. "Ms. Claire, forgive me for asking this but do you know what is going on? Gerard tells me very little when it comes to Mr. Montgomery and how he is doing. I worry so much about him. Truthfully, I worry what will happen to us once all this is over. We have lived here for so long, I don't know where we will go."

"Well, I can't answer any questions specifically about much, but I can tell you that Brian loves both you and Gerard. If I were you, I wouldn't worry too much. I have a feeling you will be well taken care of for a while."

"I know, Mr. Montgomery has been very generous to all of his staff and with no major expenditures, we have saved quite a lot over the years. But this has been my home for so long. I'm sure that sounds very selfish. But now with the lawyer here and all this gossip I hear about Peter, I am just concerned. Are we safe?"

"I think so. I can't imagine Peter would have the guts to return and threaten any of us again. I am just as confused as you are when it comes to that mess."

"I don't know Peter well, but I can tell you that this is not like him. He is usually so nice and funny when he takes all the staff out. I have only seen him angry one other time and that was a year or so ago."

That sparked Claire's interest. "What was he angry about then, or do you remember?"

"He stormed in one day and demanded that Gerard tell him where Mr. Montgomery was. The funny thing about it was Gerard thought Mr. Montgomery was with Peter on the boat. Peter pushed Gerard against the wall and threatened to punch him. Gerard was able to outmaneuver him though and told him to leave or he would call the police. Gerard yelled at him to call Mr. Montgomery on his cell because he had no idea where he was."

"Did Gerard ever tell Brian about that?"

"I don't think so. Actually if I remember correctly, Mr. Montgomery never returned to the house after that. He just left without saying goodbye or leaving instructions. By the time he returned to the compound, the incident was long forgotten."

"Hmm…" Claire thought she should ask Gerard about it when she got home.

Tank was very excited to see her and looked no worse for wear. He had a large gauze bandage on his hind leg but otherwise looked as handsome as ever. His large butt wagged back and forth when he saw her. She got down to his level and hugged him tightly. He allowed for the hug and laid his head on her shoulder, then broke away and licked her face. She got instructions from the aide and was assured that no damage other than a laceration which required a few stitches.

"If he chews off the bandage, let us know, and we will get him a cone of shame. Otherwise, he can come back in ten days to get stitches out. Try and keep him as calm as possible the next few days. The doctor ordered some pain medication for him, but he really hasn't needed it much." She handed Claire a bag with the pain meds and written instructions.

Claire walked him out and noticed there was only a slight limp. She did have to heft the eighty-five-pound dog into the car and scolded him. "It is diet time for you, buddy boy. You are getting too wide to lift!"

Tank noticed Sable, and his butt began wiggling again, almost knocking him off the back seat. He tried reaching over to lick Sable but couldn't turn easily once in the back seat. Sable reached back over the console in between and snuggled him. Claire was surprised to see tears in her eyes when she finally turned back around.

"I had no idea you were so attached to the big lug, Sable. He really is going to be fine."

"Oh yes, Ms. Claire. I love Mr. Tank even when he slobbers all over my feet while I am cooking. He is my protector, you know."

They both laughed, and Claire told Tank stories all the way back home. The whole staff was waiting at the door when they pulled up. It made Claire tear up to see how much they all loved her dog. Despite the injury, she was so happy she had brought him down for this trip. It was the first time he had ever gone to a job with her. But then she was usually home every night. She wasn't sure if she would still be alive if it weren't for Tank. The notion of him being on a diet went right out the window quickly. Everyone was lining up to give him treats and snuggles. Obviously he was in dog heaven and soaked up all the attention.

Gerard came out of the library as everyone was making a fuss and knelt down to hug Tank, too, patting him on the head as he asked Claire to join them.

When Claire walked in, Brian was awake and trying to sit on the edge of the bed. "Hey, you." She smiled. "You know you can't get up yet, right? Your legs still don't work, and the last thing I need is for you to fall and hit your head again." She turned and looked at Gerard and Harper. "I am sure he needs to perform some intimate duties. Would you two mind leaving for a few minutes? I promise not to ask or talk about anything significant in the meantime."

They looked at Claire with curious glances at first and then saw her grab a urinal and suddenly understood. They shuffled awkwardly and both left quickly. Claire chuckled to herself and assisted Brian.

"Thanks," he said. "I have been holding it for a while but didn't know how to get them out. I'm glad you realized what I needed before I said anything. Can I have something to drink?"

"Actually, Marcy made you a smoothie. Want me to get it for you?" She smiled.

"*No*! Please don't make me drink another one of her concoctions! I will pay you whatever you want, just don't make me drink it! I would like some water, please."

Claire laughed. "Okay, I am not sure how to get you out of it, but how about if I taste test one first? Some of them aren't bad at all." She handed him water and some medication.

"You aren't giving me pain medicine, are you? I need to be awake and thinking clearly for a while."

"No pain medication, and nothing that should make you sleepy, I promise. Want me to get the boys?"

"Sure. I think I am ready. Can you help me sit in a chair though? I am really getting sore, lying in bed all the time."

Claire opened the door and signaled for Harper and Gerard to come in. She and Gerard got Brian sitting in a large recliner. Claire made a mental note that Brian really needed a shower, and she really needed to check his skin closely.

"Okay, I think you should all sit down. I don't like all of you towering over me." Brian took a long drink, cleared his throat, and took another drink. "Okay. I really don't know where to begin. Gerard, would you mind taking notes?"

"Absolutely, sir." Gerard went to get pen and paper. Matthew asked Brian if he wanted the interview recorded, and Brian agreed.

They all sat quietly for a few minutes while Brian closed his eyes. The three looked at each other, fearful he had fallen back asleep. Slowly, he began.

"Awhile back, I agreed to give Rich Hughes with *Celebrity Magazine* an exclusive interview before the opening of my latest movie. He wanted to go out on the yacht. Said he had never been on one before. I agreed and called Peter and Jeff. Jeff was working for someone else and couldn't join us. Since it was just the two of us, I didn't seem too worried about just having Peter. I'm not so spoiled that I can't entertain people on my own. I offered Rich a drink once we started, and I was just drinking tea. We laughed a lot, he was easy to talk to. Everything was fine. I had told Peter before we left that I only wanted to be gone for about two hours and to turn around and head back after an hour. Anyway, we were getting along fine, and Peter came in and said he was heading back to the dock. We went up and hung out on the deck since it was such a nice night out. We noticed a few other boats nearby but didn't worry too much since they were far enough away. Rich was pretty drunk, so I told him to go into one of the guest staterooms to lie down. I started feeling sick and went into my stateroom. The next thing I remember is waking up early the next morning. We were on the dock. Peter and Rich were both gone, but the stateroom where Rich lay down had the bed unmade. I tried calling Rich but got his voice mail. I hadn't planned on being on the boat that long. I came in and grabbed my stuff and headed for the airport to catch a red eye to New York. I didn't think much of it until about a month later when nothing came out in the magazine. I called Rich's office, and they said no one had seen or heard from him in a while. The secretary said she wasn't too worried. He had taken off for months before if he was working on a hot story. Then about a week after that, I got a phone call from Peter. He said that Rich was dead and that I had killed him and began blackmailing me then. I freaked out, I couldn't remember anything. But since I didn't know what happened, I fell for it. My movie was just released, and I couldn't deal with any bad media or worse. I've been paying him monthly since. Then when we were out by that cove and I saw those boats, I started to remember things. When Marcy found those rings, I knew I needed to see them. I called Peter, and he told me to just shut up and not say anything, he would talk to me when he got rid of the boats following us. Then I passed out and woke up in the hospital. You guys know the rest of the story from there." He broke eye contact and took another drink.

Claire was the first to speak. "Brian, yesterday you said you were having dreams and remembered things. Then this morning, you mumbled something about how you could prove you didn't do it. Do you remember that?"

Brian nodded. "It's hard to know what is dream and what is reality. But I remember someone taking pictures of me, and I was... I didn't have clothes on. I remember trying to cover up but couldn't move, and everything was fuzzy. I had a horrible headache and felt sick every time I lifted my head. I remember Rich standing over me and laughing with someone else. Not Peter, not anyone I knew. He was heavy, not too tall, and had a dark beard and a camera. It's all foggy, but I remember the two of them in the salon arguing. Then I heard what sounded like a fight. That's it, that's all I remember. When I woke up, I had a raging headache and felt nauseous. I needed aspirin, and when I saw the dock, I just headed for the house. I swear I didn't kill that guy. Someone else was there, I just know it."

This time it was Harper that spoke up. "Brian, what have you been paying Peter?"

"Thirty thousand a month for the last sixteen months. I really wanted to talk to him about it, you know, clear my conscious before I die kind of thing. But I have had these nagging questions and dreams about that night. That's why I wanted to go out on the boat, and I really wanted to get Peter alone after our trip to talk to him about it, but well... I didn't get the chance. This latest letter said he wanted more money and didn't want me to call him anymore or he would go to the police. He said he had Rich's rings as proof. Matthew, show them the picture and let them hear the video."

"Are you sure you want them involved?" Harper asked.

"Yes, I am sure. I have to figure this out, and I don't know how much more time I have. I need to have answers before I die. I figure at this point, maybe it is time to call in the only cavalry. These two are a part of the cavalry."

Harper showed them a picture of the rings and a piece of clothing. The video had a bad selfie picture of Peter with the rings in his hands. He seemed nervous, cussed a lot, and said exactly what Brian had reported already. Claire couldn't help but notice that he was jerking a lot and very jittery, similar to the way he was when he cornered her on the beach. If she didn't know any better, she would think he was either on drugs or in withdrawal. She had to admit that she was partial to Brian and obviously didn't have a positive impression of

Peter, but something didn't really add up for her. Brian was sweating and turning very pale; his hand had slight tremors.

"I am sorry to interrupt at a bad time, but I really feel like we need to get Brian back to bed, and I need to get him pain medication." Claire stood and went to get medicine and the wheelchair. She and Gerard got Brian back into bed, and she took his vital signs. Harper paced in the background and scribbled notes on a pad. Brian fought to keep his eyes open and held on to Claire's hand. "You believe me, don't you? I didn't kill that guy. I just know it."

"Actually, Brian, I do believe you. Rest now and let these guys do their job. I have faith in them, and I have faith in you too. We will get answers for you." He squeezed her hand and closed his eyes.

Once Brian was asleep, the other three congregated in Gerard's office. "Claire, I need more than just a few minutes with Brian. I also need him clearheaded and not looking half-dead already so we can make a deposition just in case anything happens before he… well you know. Is that going to be possible?"

"I really don't know, Mr. Harper. Part of his sleeping so much is just his normal decline, but it will be difficult to know how much is related to his subdural hematoma. I personally don't recommend him going in for more testing. The most recent scan showed that no cancer had gone to his brain, so that should be helpful to you, right? It shows he is still cognitive."

"Claire, we have known each other a long time. Please stop calling me Mr. Harper and just call me Matthew. And yes, it helps. I have already contacted my private investigator to come down and replace me. I really need to get back to London. Would you guys mind giving me a few minutes to make some calls?"

"Of course, Mr. Harper. I will make sure Sable has your clothes washed, packed, and ready to go. I think Marcy was making something to eat as well. Can I help with any calls?"

"No, Gerard, you have all been wonderful. Thank you so much. Please call me Matthew as well, and while I am here, it might be a good time to get you both to sign Brian's will and get his estate in order. I was going to email him and let him know that the Los Angeles property had sold at a nice profit, and I adjusted his paperwork accordingly. I just need to call the pilot and give him a flight plan. Since it is getting late and I am hoping to talk to Brian once more, I will probably plan on leaving tomorrow around noon."

"Yes, sir. I will make sure everything is prepared." Gerard turned and left while Claire was chewing on a nail and staring at her feet.

"Claire? Would you mind?"

"What? Oh yes, sorry. I just kept remembering that Brian mentioned a man with a beard, not very tall... I can't help but think I may know who he is talking about, but I will have to remember where I have seen him. I will leave you alone and let you know when dinner is ready. Would you like to eat in the formal dining room?"

"It doesn't matter much to me, I am used to eating in very informal spaces like my desk, my lap, in the car... I am not picky." Matthew chuckled.

Claire headed for the kitchen to see if she could help but couldn't get that description of a man out of her head. Marcy and Sable assured Claire they had dinner preparations under control, and Marcy suggested a swim or a walk with Tank.

"Actually, both are great ideas. Maybe a short walk with Tank while he is recovering, and then he can hang out with me while I swim. Thanks, Marcy!"

Claire got the leash, a few treats, and the doggie poo bag, and she and Tank headed out. Claire kept a watchful eye on his gait and felt secure enough to take him to the fountain—his favorite place. They walked a slower pace than normal, and Claire noticed him panting a little harder than normal with long strips of thick drool falling off his jowls. He really wanted to jump in, but she held him back, not wanting to get his wound wet. They walked the short distance to the guesthouse, and she got him fresh water.

She walked back to the room she had been staying in and realized all of her clothes had been moved to the main house. She checked Marcy's room, but it was empty as well. She was really disappointed since she really wanted to relax with a swim. A mischievous smile crossed her face as she made sure all the doors were locked and the blinds were closed. She looked at Tank and said, "I haven't been skinny-dipping since I was a young girl, but what's a lady to do? We need to keep this a secret. Deal?"

Confident Tank would keep the secret, she took off her clothes and jumped in. The water was so warm and relaxing. She swam hard for twenty or thirty minutes, then leaned back and floated mindlessly. Her eyes were closed when she suddenly remembered where she had seen that man. Her eyes opened wide, and she smiled. "I got it Tank! I know where I have seen him!" She splashed the dog and decided to do another few laps. When she started to get out, she screamed as she saw two figures walking towards her. Gerard was carrying the bags of some man she had never met, and he was giving him the same tour of the house that Marcy and she had gotten when they first arrived. She frantically looked for a towel or her clothes, but they were on the far side of the patio. She plastered herself as close to the edge of the pool and yelled at Gerard not to come in. Too late. He opened the patio door and stopped still in his tracks. His companion raised his eyebrows and smiled. "Well, Gerard, I must say the amenities and scenery are outstanding."

Gerard's face was beet red as he tried to block himself between the guest and Claire. Claire didn't dare move away but was almost in tears from embarrassment. "Gerard, please!"

Gerard stuttered, "I'm sorry, Ms. Claire. I had no idea you would be here. I thought since you and Ms. Marcy had moved to the main house, it would be alright for Mr. Jack to stay here. I... I had no idea."

The two of them continued to stand and gawk at Claire, not knowing what to do. Claire was humiliated and nearly cried. "Gerard, please leave. I will meet you at the main house and explain."

"Yes, ma'am. I'm sorry, ma'am."

"You might be sorry, mate, but I am rather enjoying myself. Can I get you a towel, my lady?" Jack laughed.

"No, you may not!" Claire said forcefully. "You may leave like you were asked!"

Once they were gone, Claire got out and dried off. She glared at Tank. "What kind of guard dog are you? You could have warned me!" Tank tilted his head and wagged his nub of a tail, tongue out, and drooling. "I'm sorry, buddy, not your fault. Lord, forgive me. I don't know what I was thinking." She looked at Tank and cried. "How am I ever going to look those two in the eye? All I wanted was a peaceful, relaxing swim!"

She quickly dressed but really did not want to head to the main house. She paced around the front of the house for a while, trying to decide if she wanted to pretend it never happened and waltz into the front unapologetic or sneak into the back trying to hide from everyone. She opted for the latter. She slid in the backdoor and passed Gerard's office. She peeked in on Brian who was still sleeping. She rounded the corner hall into the kitchen as Sable, Marcy, Gerard, and the guest were all making introductions. She tried to back out quietly, but Marcy spotted her. "There's Claire. Claire, this is Matthew's private investigator, Jack Presley. He looks like he and Elvis could be related, huh?"

Claire didn't bother to look up. "Claire and I have already met, but thank you, Marcy," Jack interjected. "Actually, I have met every beautiful inch of Claire." He grabbed Claire's hand and lightly kissed her knuckles. "Beautiful name, beautiful body… how could a man get so lucky? Please tell me you are single."

Claire jerked her hand back and stuck both of her hands in her pocket, not saying a word for fear she would burst into tears.

Marcy looked at Claire and Gerard whose cheeks were cherry red, and both were looking at the floor. She looked at Jack who looked like a little boy presented a prize trophy. "Excuse me? You just got here, can someone tell me what in the Sam Hill is going on here?"

Jack chuckled. "Let's just say I am a gentleman who doesn't kiss and tell. Or in this case, gaze and tell."

Marcy looked at Claire. "You had best tell me what's going on here!"

Just then, Matthew walked in and interrupted the awkward moment. Claire signaled to Gerard to be quiet and glared at Marcy shaking her head no. Matthew walked over to Jack and grabbed him in a big bear-hug. None of the group besides Jack had ever seen Matthew in anything other than a professional manner. They were surprised to see him relaxed, casual, and looking like a little boy who had just found his long-lost best friend.

"Oh, man, buddy, is it good to see your ugly mug," he gushed, not completely letting go.

Jack returned the sentiment. "It's been a while, friend. Last time I saw you was in Peru, wasn't it? Getting back that old hag's ugly paintings, right?"

Matthew nodded. "Yes, but we can't discuss any more of that case here and now. Follow me, I will catch you up with what I know before dinner."

The two headed back to Gerard's office. When they were gone, Marcy and Sable looked at Claire and Gerard with their brows cued up and arms crossed across their chests.

Gerard cleared his throat. "I suppose I will get the rest of Mr. Presley's things into the guesthouse." He glanced at Claire and had a hard time not smiling or laughing.

"Spill it, sister!" Marcy demanded.

"I can't, I am humiliated, okay? That should make you happy!" Claire cried.

"Bull hockey, spill it!"

"I just wanted to take a swim, and the guesthouse pool was so close and private. I forgot that all of our belongings are now up here. I just wanted a swim, I swear! I had no idea that those two would burst in there! I just wanted a swim!"

"Claire, stop babbling. We get it. You wanted a swim, so what's the big deal?" Marcy questioned.

"I didn't have a swimsuit, but no one was around, so I... I... just drop it, Marcy, would you!" She turned and headed up the stairs. Marcy and Sable watched her leave, looked at each other, and burst out laughing. Claire heard their cackling as she hit the top of the stairs, and she bolted into her room to cry.

Dinner was awkward to say the least. Poor Matthew had no idea what all the giggles and silly looks were about but decided he didn't have the time or inclination to find out. Halfway through dinner, Claire remembered her epiphany in the pool. "Matthew, when you are finished eating, could I talk to you for a minute?"

"Sure, Claire. Dinner was delicious, Sable. But I feel like the odd man out on a dirty secret, so I think I am done for the night. Gerard, do you want to meet in your study so we can sign those papers?"

"Certainly, sir. I will join you in a few minutes."

Matthew and Claire walked back to the study. "Okay, I might be crazy tired, but am I missing something? Dinner was strange."

"Never mind that, Matthew. I think I remember something. Remember when Brian said there was someone else on the boat? His description of the man kept nagging at me until I remembered that I saw a man who matches that same description when we were on the boat that day. He was in another boat that was following us and taking pictures. Brian didn't seem to react much when he saw the man though, so maybe I'm wrong. But the description Brian gave was dead-on of this guy."

"It's a start anyway. Do you think you could describe him to Jack? Maybe have the others see if they remember him too?" Matthew asked.

"I suppose... will he be leaving with you in the morning?" Claire prayed silently.

"No, Jack is staying to investigate Brian's story and see if he can find Peter." Matthew noticed a look of what he thought might be fear on Claire's face. "Don't worry, I've known Jack for years and trust him with my life. He's a great guy, trust me."

"I'm sure he is, it's just... oh, never mind. It's fine, Matthew. I am going to check in on Brian." She turned to leave as Jack and Gerard were heading in, and she literally ran straight into Jack, stumbled back a little, and he reached out to grab her, drawing her close to him.

"We really were made to be together, weren't we?" Jack chuckled.

"Excuse me, I need to go see my patient," she mumbled and bolted out the door.

Jack and Gerard couldn't help but smile. Matthew stood behind the desk with his hands out. "Can someone fill me in? What is up with you two?"

Gerard clasped his hands behind his back and bit his lower lip. Jack just shrugged and said, "No worries, mate, just a little embarrassing story of how I met the beautiful lass. She probably would prefer I kept it to myself though."

"Geez, Jack! Can't you just this once keep women off your mind and concentrate on the case? You better watch it with her, you are going to need her on this one. Plus I don't think she is interested in romance right now."

"Ahhh, come on, mate. You know me better than that, I can handle a woman and the case at the same time. Plus the only reason she isn't interested is because she doesn't know me yet," he said with a chuckle.

"I'm serious, Jack. She just lost her husband, and it wasn't pretty. It was pretty devastating to her actually."

"Oh well, I suppose that's another story. How long ago?"

"Um... I think it's been two, no, five years ago. Wow, doesn't seem like that long."

"Time flies the older we get, mate, and five years for a lassie as fine as that one is long enough. Trust me, usually at that age, they are looking to replace after a year."

"Not her. Look, Jack, enough about Claire. Let me fill you in on what I know so far. I have to get back to London tomorrow, and I need to take care of some other things before I leave." They discussed the situation for another hour, and Matthew gave Jack the pictures, flash drive, envelope, and copied him in on the video he made with Brian earlier that day.

Gerard brought them in dessert and coffee. Matthew asked Gerard to stay and review the will and estate paperwork while he took Jack in to meet Brian.

When they walked into the library, Brian was sleeping, and Claire was reading softly to him. She looked up smiled at Matthew and blushed when she saw Jack. "Lassie, the color looks good on ya, but trust me, yours is not the first naked body I have seen and, by God in heaven, I pray not the last. There is no sense in your being embarrassed every time you see me. We are going to have to work together pretty closely, so I reckon it is time you get over yourself."

Claire just stood and turned away. "You are right, Mr. Presley." She began fussing with Brian's blankets. "Matthew, is there anything you need from me before I turn in?"

"No, Claire, thanks." She started out the door when he said, "Oh wait, Claire! Yes, I do need you to witness Gerard's signature on some papers. Are you still willing to do that?"

"Of course. I will meet you in Gerard's study then. Good night, Mr. Presley."

"Might as well knock off the Mr. nonsense, Claire. Have a good night, I will see you in the morning to review the case. Sweet dreams, my Claire. I know mine will be sweet tonight."

He let out an "oomph" when Matthew shoved his elbow into his ribs. "What did I say now?" He looked at Matthew, smiling.

"I'll see you in a few minutes, Claire, thank you." Matthew glared at Jack as he said it.

"Why don't you go after Marcy instead?" Matthew said after Claire left. "She's more your style anyway. You know, fly by night, impulsive, free-minded, and an idiot when it comes to relationships."

"Ah, lad, are you ever going to give in and let your heart lead for once instead of wrapping that brilliant mind in work all the time? Trust me, lad, you are the last one to give relationship advice to anyone. When was the last time ya kissed a girl?"

"It's been... hey, don't turn this on me! I am perfectly happy with my life right now." He turned and looked at Brian. He shook his shoulders a little but got no response. "Well, looks like you aren't going to meet him tonight. Hopefully he will wake up a little in the morning."

"What's wrong with him?" Jack stood back as if Brian was contagious.

"Cancer. He isn't long for this world, I'm afraid." Jack relaxed a little. "Don't worry, Jack, I am sure you can get an autograph for your portfolio before he goes. Especially if you figure out exactly what happened that night and get this creep off his back."

"I'll do my best, mate."

"I know you will. There are few I trust to get the information I need before I turn this over to the authorities. I have worked with

Brian for a long time. He was my first client at the firm as a matter of fact. He is brilliant, but like most creative geniuses, he's been a jerk a lot of the time. He always treated me with respect though. You two will either get along great, or you will be like oil and water. For his sake, I hope it's the first. He needs you, and he needs you at your best."

"I told ya, I got this one. Quit worrying, mate. It puts lines on that handsome face, and it doesn't become ya."

"Okay. I am going to check in on Gerard to see if he has questions, then head to my room to catch up on calls. You good for the night?"

"Right as rain, mate. G'night. And hey, it's good to see you. It's been too long."

"I agree. It's good to see you too." They hugged and slapped each other on the back and then headed separate ways.

Gerard looked as if he was in shock when Matthew walked in. "I can't sign this, sir. It's too generous. What is he thinking? He must have gone mad! The cancer must have gone to his brain."

Matthew smiled and squeezed Gerard's shoulder. "The basics have been this way for years, Gerard. Long before he was diagnosed. If you don't believe me, I can show you his previous will that was written several years ago."

"He didn't even hint that he liked us until a few weeks ago! I feel terrible for every bad word I said against him."

"You have been incredibly loyal, and he respects you and Sable very much. He even told me a long time ago you were like the brother he never had."

"But he never acted like that! How can he say that?"

"Don't look a gift horse in the mouth, Gerard. You deserve every dime. Any questions about the provisions?"

"Not right now, sir. I think I am still in shock a little."

"Take some time to talk to Sable about all this, and I will see you both in the morning." Matthew gave them both a short wave and left quietly while Gerard was still reading.

Claire was off in her own world, sitting in a corner, watching the sunset. It was still very warm outside, and Claire longed to be out there instead of in the house. She asked Gerard if he needed anything. "I am sure you are going to want to discuss all of this with Sable and ask Matthew some questions before you sign that, so I am heading outside for a bit after I check on Brian for the night, is that okay?" Claire asked. Gerard nodded his head not really hearing what she said.

Claire checked on Brian and did her nightly duties. He grunted a little as she adjusted pillows and made sure his sheets were dry and clean. His vital signs were all normal, his skin was remarkably good. She felt safe leaving him for the night but would alert Sable just in case. Their quarters were much closer than her room upstairs; and although there was a cot set up for her in the library, she really wanted to sleep in a real bed tonight. She would talk to Gerard tomorrow about transferring Brian back up to his room upstairs tomorrow. They could weigh the pros and cons, and if they kept him downstairs, maybe they could work out better sleeping arrangements for her. She found Marcy, Sable, and Jack on the porch, eating strawberries and ice cream. She hesitated before walking out there but realized that Jack was probably right about her getting over herself. She had seen plenty of naked men and never flinched, it was part of her job. This felt different, only because she was the one with no clothes, and she didn't feel humiliated around Gerard now. She needed to just shake it off and deal with the situation.

She walked out, hoping that her cheeks weren't red, smiled at Marcy and Sable, and kept her eyes far away from Jack Presley for now. She told Sable that Brian was sleeping alone in the library, Gerard was in his study, and Matthew was upstairs in his room, making calls but didn't expect him back down for the night. She asked Marcy if she wanted to go for a walk with her down by the beach. Jack jumped up. "I could stretch my legs some, get rid of the ice cream calories, and ask you some questions about Peter if you don't mind me walking with you two."

"I'm not really up for it tonight, Claire." Marcy winked at her. "I trust Jack here to keep you safe… at least from creeps like Peter anyway."

Claire shot Marcy a glare which only made Marcy laugh. "It's all right, love. You don't need a chaperone or a curfew but know that I will wait up for you." Jack gently grabbed Claire's elbow with one hand and made a wide gesture with the other for her to lead. He threw Marcy and Sable a wink as they walked back into the house.

"You know, I really am tired. Maybe I will just head up to bed." Claire tried to dodge out of the walk.

"Maybe you need a swim instead?" Jack chided her.

"How about if I stop acting embarrassed around you, and you never mention or tease me about it, deal?" she said through a forced smile.

"Ah, lovely Claire. No need to be embarrassed, but that beautiful memory will be etched in my mind for quite a long time. And it's up to you, but I promise to be a gentleman. And I really would like to ask you questions about the case."

Claire shrugged her shoulders. She really wasn't afraid of him, and maybe she could get over her embarrassment easier if they actually did talk about the case instead of how they met.

"You have an interesting accent, Jack. Where are you from?" she asked as she led him out the back gate toward the beach.

"My folks had a serious case of wanderlust. I lived in Scotland, Ireland, New Zealand, and five states here in America, all before I was sixteen. I speak six languages, but I am afraid I don't speak all of them well. I tend to flow from one to another. Forgive me."

"Nothing to forgive. I didn't say I didn't like it, I said it was interesting," she said, smiling.

"Ah, lassie, I knew ya had a thing for me." He nudged her with his shoulder and winked. "But seriously, tell me everything you remember about that day on the boat and then the day with Peter. Don't leave anything out."

Claire recanted the whole story again, trying hard to remember it all. She felt like she should just record it so she wouldn't have to repeat it over and over. She had a bad feeling this wouldn't be her last time telling the story. She did tell Jack about Brian's description of the man on the boat the night of the supposed murder, matching the description of the man on the boat following them that day. When she was done, she looked up and noticed that they were far from the house, and it was completely dark. The moon was bright; it was still very warm, but there was a light breeze, cooled by the ocean.

She stopped, closed her eyes, and took a deep breath. She could always rely on the ocean to give her some peace. She didn't realize until that moment how much she missed her morning yoga, prayer, and time alone in the mornings at home. She was so lost in thought she had forgotten Jack was standing beside her until he gently put his arm around her. She started to lean into him as she would have Dirk and then suddenly jerked away.

"Lovely Claire, don't waste a beautiful moment by getting all freaky on me."

"I'm sorry. Look, I don't want to be rude, but I am not interested in a romantic relationship. I would appreciate it if you would keep that in mind. Technically I may be single, but in my heart, I am still married. I lost my husband five years ago, but some days, it feels like yesterday."

"I hear you, but I don't believe you. No one as lovely as you should be alone. You deserve to be treated like a queen."

Claire laughed. "Wow, now it's you who is unbelievable. I wouldn't consider myself as lovely as you say. You obviously have charmed plenty with that hogwash, but I am not some gullible young filly looking for a stud."

He stopped, grabbed her hand, and turned her around to face him. He brushed her cheek gently then framed his large hands around her face. "May God strike me dead if I am lying about just how lovely you are. It isn't in how you look on the outside, although I admit, it is pleasing. It is a certain aura you emit that makes you lovely."

He was careful not to kiss her like he wanted to, but he couldn't resist drawing her closer. He wrapped his arms around her and was pleasantly surprised when she didn't pull away immediately. "I'll bide my time and promise never to push you too hard, my love. But promise you won't push away too quickly either."

She did lean into him, remembering how good it felt. He was taller and broader than Dirk, it felt comforting. And she hadn't realized just how badly she missed the simple act of being held. They both were silent for a few moments; but when he pulled back enough to try and kiss her, she broke away. She didn't say anything but did take his hand and began walking back to the house. She wasn't ready for this, but her heart was beating quickly. She needed to be safely in her room and far away from Jack Presley for a while. She walked a little faster on the way back and tried to keep her mind off him matching her gait step for step. They remained silent on the walk back, and by the time they reached the house, they were almost jogging. As they reached the backstairs, Jack pulled her a little closer and kissed her forehead.

"Good night, lovely Claire. It's my turn to take a swim, and I pray the water is cold. Feel free to stop by if you are interested in turning the tables on the view later."

"Good night, Jack. I will see you tomorrow," Claire answered softly but firmly.

Gerard and Sable's door was closed with a soft light escaping underneath. Brian was snoring loudly and seemed quite peaceful. Marcy was reading a book on the porch swing with Tank curled up and sleeping beside her. When she saw Claire, she set her book down and indicated for Claire to sit in the chair across from her. "Tell me everything."

"I'm not sure I can. He's handsome in a rugged sort of way and charming, but I just don't think I am ready. And I definitely don't want to be in a fly-by-night relationship which I am sure all he is looking for. Sorry to disappoint you, my friend. But no match making here, I'm afraid."

Marcy wanted so badly to argue with her, but she knew it was fruitless right now, so she just smiled and squeezed Claire's hand. "I understand, my friend. Just promise you will allow yourself to be open to signals from Dirk and God when the time is right to love again."

Claire laughed. "I don't think I will be seeing signs from Dirk. He may not have been the jealous type, but I don't think he would be pushing me into another relationship either."

"You might be right, trust God then to let you know," Marcy teased.

"Look who's talking. Ernesto follows you around like a puppy in heat, yet you just ignore him!" Claire shot back.

Marcy hugged her friend and laughed. "Playing hard to get... it's been fun. I haven't been courted like this in years."

Claire headed up to bed, feeling a little lighter. She pulled out her Bible and found the rose she had pressed into the pages in Songs of Solomon. She gently lifted the rose and kissed it. "No one can take your place, Dirk, don't worry."

Claire woke up at 5:00 a.m., and for the first time in weeks, she went out for yoga and an early morning swim. She was reading her daily devotional when Sable came out and let her know that Brian was awake. She grabbed one of Marcy's smoothies from the fridge and headed into the library. Matthew was in with Brian, and they were smiling when she walked in.

"You look wide awake and great, buddy. How do you feel?" Claire asked.

"Not bad, the fogginess is starting to fade a little. I still feel dizzy when I try to stand, and I don't feel like my legs work. But the pain isn't horrible yet."

"Brian, we talked about this. Please don't try to get up by yourself yet. Someone needs to be in here with you."

"Someone was with me, Mother Hen. Matt was here."

"Here." She handed him the smoothie. "Marcy is getting better with her recipes. The latest batch actually taste really good."

"No, thanks. I am hungry though, feels good to say that."

"Scaredy-cat. Just take one drink and if you don't like it, you don't have to finish it."

"Yes, Mommy." Brian laughed and took a tiny sip. "Actually you're right, it's tasty." He chugged the rest quickly, licked his lips, and asked if there was more.

"How about we see how well that stays down. And if you are still hungry in a bit, I will whip up some eggs."

"Sounds heavenly," he said, smiling.

"What is up with you today? You are almost giggling! This isn't the Brian Montgomery I know. Want to fill me in?"

"I know I didn't do that murder. I've been paying off that idiot for way too long, and I just feel like a huge weight has been lifted off my shoulders."

"That's great! How do you know?" Claire was relieved.

"I just do. You guys will have to prove it, but I just have this peaceful feeling. For the longest time, I have carried this guilt, thinking I must have done it and Peter must have proof. The truth is, he never said he saw me do it. The rings don't mean anything, and he is assuming I did it. I should have gone to Matthew when this first happened. We could have investigated this a lot sooner and saved me a lot of money."

"Well, I am willing to do whatever I can to help, but I'm not a detective. I'm not sure how helpful I can be on that end especially since I didn't even know you then."

"Yeah, no offense, Claire, but I feel better with Matt and Jack helping. I can't explain it, but I feel great today and want to get involved. Do you think you can help me stand up?"

"We can try but, Brian, you need to go slowly. You haven't walked in a while, and your muscles have gotten a lot weaker. Let me get some help first, okay?"

"I can help," Matthew said. "Here, grab my arm."

"Just wait a second, you two. Someone needs to be on each side and someone to stand behind with the wheelchair." Claire turned to get help as Jack walked in the door.

"Perfect timing," Matthew said. "Grab an arm, and, Claire, you can stand behind with the chair."

Once they were all in position, Brian stood and took a few steps. He was weak and wobbly but able to walk to the bathroom across the hall. Sable and Gerard brought in trays with breakfast while Brian was in the bathroom and by the time he came out, the whole crew was there applauding as he walked back to the library without help.

Brian blushed but had to admit he was pretty happy with himself. He hadn't felt this good in a very long time and wanted to savor every moment.

"Hey, mate, I'm pleased you are feeling better. But are you willing to answer some questions and let me earn my keep?" Jack asked.

"Sure, I know you already know most of the story. I feel like I have repeated it a million times in the last few days. What else do you want to know?" Brian sat at the desk and dived into breakfast.

"Do you remember more about the actual night with the reporter lad? You said you vaguely remember another person there but couldn't be clear." Jack pulled out a small notebook and made notes.

"I do remember a little. He was dressed in black, like a wet suit. He was tall and had a beard. I didn't know who he was and was startled to see him there because as far as I know, he appeared out of nowhere."

"Okay, mate. Now how many drinks did you have that night?" Jack asked.

"Actually, I was drinking iced tea. I had been clean and sober for a while, but yeah, I can remember feeling the same way I did after a binger. I felt sick to my stomach, and everything was blurry. I remember the beginning of the night really clearly. But once we were out for a couple hours, everything feels like it is foggy and in slow motion."

"Did your reporter friend know you were sober?"

"I am pretty sure he did, he was drinking beer. He made a comment about how ironic it was that I own a winery and a brewery but never get to sample the goods."

"Okay, do you think you were drugged?"

"I don't know that for sure, but it all went blurry pretty quickly. It would explain a lot."

"Do you think Peter was in on it with them or just the reporter? What was his name? Ah... Richard Hughes and stranger?"

"I have no idea, but why would he?"

"Well, that's where I am starting. I need to know more about Peter. Do you have employment history on him?"

"Actually not much. Peter and Luke are contracted workers. They work for a lot of people down here, but I will get you all the information I do have."

Matthew spoke up. "I have already given him what I have in our files. Do you have anything else?"

"No, sorry. I am sure we have the same." Brian looked a little dejected for the first time that morning.

"Claire said there was a man that fit the description of the stranger on another boat the day you all went out. Do you remember that?" Jack asked.

"I didn't pay much attention really. I try to avoid paparazzi and didn't want to look their way. I went into my stateroom where cameras can't see anything. The lounge has a lot of glass and is not exactly the most private."

"Okay, well, I am going out with Marcy, Claire, and Ernesto this afternoon to see if I can get anything from the boat."

"Why do you need them to go? I don't really think they can help you much."

"Ernesto can guide us to the cove where Marcy found those rings. I am not the most experienced diver and can use some help."

"Okay, that explains Marcy and Ernesto but why Claire? And who are you going to use as a captain? Peter was the only one who has ever been contracted for the yacht."

"I can drive it, and I am taking Luke with me too if that's okay."

"Maybe I should go, too, then. It might help me remember."

"Are you sure you're up for that, mate?" Jack wasn't sure he could drive the boat, do his job, and be nursemaid all at the same time.

"I think so." Brian looked at Claire. "What do you think?"

"I don't advise it. I would prefer you wait a few days and see if this sudden change of condition holds up."

Claire didn't want to discourage him, but she had questions about his safety.

"But what if it doesn't hold up, and I have wasted a good day lying in bed when I could help?"

Claire had to admit he had a good point and shrugged her shoulders. Let's get your vitals, and I will call the doctor and let him decide.

Matthew stood and said, "For what it's worth, I think Brian should go. I wish I could be here to assist, but I need to leave within the hour. I will call you when I get to London. Brian, don't be stupid, and if the doctor says it isn't a good idea, then we will come up with something else. We all want answers, let us help. Got it?"

Brian saluted and smiled at Matthew. "Yes, sir!"

He reached to shake Matthew's hand. "Seriously, thank you for being here. You have no idea what it means to me."

Matthew smiled and hugged him. "Whatever you need, man. You were my first client, and you have pretty much paid most of my student loans over the years. Whatever I can do to help, you just let me know. I just wish you had come to me sooner. As it is, I don't really feel comfortable keeping all this from the authorities. I am giving Jack one week to come up with a complete story, and then we will all have to face the music, brother."

"Deal. I just hope Jack is as good as all the stories I have heard over the years." Brian smiled but started to worry how much they could get answered in one week.

Matthew met with Jack in private while Claire did her assessment on Brian.

"Do you have any of your gut feelings yet?" Matthew asked Jack.

"I do, but I don't want to divulge too soon." Jack smiled.

"Well, just be sure that you go with the gut feelings and not the ones you get lower when you look at Claire. I mean it, Jack. I need you on your A game for this one."

"No need to worry, Chief. I never let the hens interfere with the job. You should know that by now." Jack would've been offended if that had come from anyone but Matt. He knew how important Brian Montgomery was to Matthew though, so he let it slide.

"Good. I wouldn't trust this case with anyone else. Just be sure to give me daily updates, okay?"

"Will do. Godspeed to London, mate."

Two hours later, they were packed and loading on the yacht. Claire had a bad déjà vu feeling and couldn't imagine what Brian was feeling. She sent a signal to Gerard to check Brian's stateroom to see if it had been cleaned yet. She didn't want Brian to see the blood and mess from the last time he was here. Gerard came back, cheeks red, and shook his head no. Thankfully, at least for now, Brian wanted to stay in the lounge and showed no interest in going back there. Jack came up behind Claire and asked her to join him on the bridge.

"I need you to take diligent notes since I can't be down there questioning him and steering the boat at the same time. I need him to walk through that night as much as possible. Ernesto is staying up here with me and Luke to guide us to the cove. Once we anchor, you and Marcy can dive to see if there is any other evidence in the surrounding area. Do you have all the supplies you need before we head out?"

"I'm pretty sure we do. Maybe Gerard should dive with us too since he knows the area well. Let me make sure we have enough tanks." She left as the other three mapped out a course.

Claire checked supplies and asked Gerard about diving with them. She was glad that for the time being, Sable and Marcy were hovering over Brian to ensure he was comfortable. Maybe it was the boat, but Claire had that same nagging feeling and prayed silently that this whole idea wasn't a huge mistake. Brian felt good today but wouldn't survive another fall like the last one. She turned to head back into the lounge as a tall lanky young man came running up to the bridge.

"Mr. Presley?" Jack turned and looked.

"Yes, I'm Jack Presley. Who are you?"

"My name is Steve, and Mr. Montgomery hired me to captain the boat." Steve nodded at Jack.

Claire almost laughed as Jack looked awkward, not knowing what was going on. "He doesn't trust me with his fancy boat, huh?" He looked angrily at the boy.

"Ahhh, I don't know, sir. I just know I am supposed to take over. You'll have to talk to Mr. Montgomery if you have questions." He blushed.

"It's all right, lad. I'd prefer to be down there anyway." Jack chuckled and patted the boy on the back. "Don't run her aground for me, would ya?"

Steve smiled. "Yes, sir."

He slid into Jack's spot, and Jack threw his arm around Claire's waist. "I guess you won't have to take notes after all." He pulled her close and kissed her forehead. Claire's face turned instantly red, and she pulled herself away.

Down in the lounge, Brian looked at Jack coming in and was prepared for an argument. Luckily Jack didn't seem to mind the sudden change of plans, and Brian was relieved. Truth was, Brian didn't trust many people to drive his boat. Once he knew they were going out, he called his friend who gave Steve a good reference, and he got really lucky that Steve was available. Brian knew Jack was a great detective, but he didn't know how well he could handle a vessel this size.

"Okay, let's get to work." Jack started. "I know you have all been through the story multiple times. But now that we are here, I want all of you to close your eyes and go through every detail. Brian, we can start with you first, and I know it will be tough, but I want you to imagine everything that happened that night. I have notes here and can add any small detail you might have forgotten."

Brian leaned back and tried to remember. Everything was fuzzy that night after he had a drink. Jack suspected that he was drugged at some point. One common denominator from both Brian and Claire's story was a man of similar build and looks. Jack would have to use one of his resources to see if the profile sketch would match in a facial recognition database. Gerard came down and said they were nearing the cove where Marcy found the rings. The weather was warm but cloudy, and a soft rain had started. Jack asked Claire if she was ready to dive.

"You have plenty of people helping. I'm sure you don't really need me. And I think I would like to stay with Brian if that's okay," Claire remarked.

Jack shrugged his shoulders and noticed Marcy was all geared up and ready to go. "I guess I will have to settle for another beautiful date today," Jack teased.

"Ha!" Marcy laughed. "You couldn't handle me as a date, buddy boy. Although it might be kinda nice to see if Ernesto would get a little jealous. Lucky for you, I am too dang old to play those games anymore. Come on, lightweight, let's rock and roll. I will take you to the area, and you can help me move some rocks around. But be careful, there are a lot of corals over there, too, and I don't want you to touch it and end up killing it all."

"Don't worry, love. This isn't my first time-out." Jack winked as he pulled on his wet suit. "How deep is it? Do we need tanks or is it shallow enough for just snorkel gear?"

"We didn't have tanks before," Marcy said. "There is a little cavern-like area just beyond that I didn't explore, and I am not sure if we will need tanks in there though. See if Gerard or Ernesto think we need tanks, they are more familiar of the area."

Both Gerard and Ernesto came in suited up just as Jack was heading up. They all stood on the deck and mapped out where they could split up and look. Two of them took tanks while the other two were going to snorkel and scope out a wider area. Claire made herself busy in one of the staterooms until they all dove off. She really would have liked to go with them, but she needed a break from Jack.

She fussed over Brian for a while, and they both were lost in their own thoughts. It was nice to just have some silence. "So what's up with you and Jack?" Brian finally asked.

"I'm not sure I know what you mean, there isn't anything going on with me and Jack." Claire wouldn't turn and look at him, she kept her back to him and pretended like she was busy prepping medications.

"Don't lie to me, Claire. You don't owe me any explanations, but I thought we were friends at least." Brian's voice was a little harsher than he intended.

"I'm not lying, Brian. He may wish there were something more going on, but I am not interested in the type of relationship that men like you and Jack are interested in." Her back instinctively straightened, and she found herself getting a little more defensive than she would have liked.

"How do you know what type of relationship we want? Why is it women always think all men want is a quick roll in the hay? I mean, sure, when I was in my twenties and thirties, I may have not wanted more than that. But we do get wiser as we get older, you know! Besides, you don't put off that kind of vibe anyway."

This made Claire smile and relax a little. "Exactly what kind of vibe do I give off then?"

"More like a Sunday-school-teacher vibe. Definitely a good girl vibe, but that kind of makes you more irresistible in a way. Men like to see if they can make the good girl turn into a bad girl. Be careful. I don't really know what kind of women Jack is interested in, but I actually do agree with you a little. I am not sure he is prepared for a long-term relationship, but I don't want to see you getting hurt." Claire noticed that his voice was a little sad. She wondered if he had regrets about his past relationships.

"You don't need to worry, Brian. I am not interested in any type of relationship other than friendship right now. I have already had a wonderful marriage and love. I like being single, and I have no desire to get entangled with anyone like that at this point in my life." Claire smiled. She wasn't lying. She really was happy and wasn't about to throw a monkey wrench like love into her life.

"Well, you better be sure to let him know that. He definitely has the hots for you, and you two look way too comfy together. I think you are more attached than you are willing to admit." Claire shot him a dirty look, and he laughed and just held up both hands. "Hey, just saying. But yeah, I can back off for now. Do you think there is really anything down there to find after all this time?"

"I doubt it, really. I don't like the look of the skies though. Hopefully they don't spend too much time out there. They should've all taken tanks just in case."

"They are all experienced, don't be such a mother hen. I just worry this is all pointless. I wish I could remember more from that night." Brian yawned. Claire looked at him and felt such pity. She wished that she could help more.

"Why don't you try to rest? Jack may want to grill you again when they get back." Claire suggested. She was actually feeling very tired herself. Unfortunately, a nap was not in her near future. She wanted to review Jack's notes and see if there was anything they might have missed.

The group came back on board about two hours later, looking worn out and worried. They took off their wet suits and entered the lounge without saying a word. Brian and Claire could tell that the news was not hopeful. Claire gave Marcy a questioning look, and Marcy just bowed her head and shook it no.

Sensing that no one was in the mood to chat, Claire poured the group a glass of wine and Brian a glass of sparkling water. She also pulled out a couple of meat/cheese platters that she had put together while they were out. They quickly went through three bottles of wine before anyone was willing to talk.

"Okay, time to regroup." Jack cleared his throat and tried to sound more positive than he felt. I think I want to focus on finding the mystery third bloke that you remembered Brian. Claire, you said it might be the same guy that was following the yacht. The supposed victim was a member of the press, so maybe he is too."

"Sounds logical. Maybe I could use some of my resources to find out." Brian nodded. He took a picture of the sketch and sent it with an email to his publicist and agent. Although the day didn't give them the answers they were hoping for, they were starting to relax and decided to head back. A storm was brewing, and the water was choppy. Jack silently said a thank-you prayer that he wasn't having to steer in rough weather.

By the time they docked, they were all exhausted. Dinner was a quiet affair, and they all went to their separate quarters early. Tank could feel the tension and stuck close to Claire. Claire was both relieved and disappointed that Jack didn't say much to her all day. She decided to take advantage of the quiet, grabbed Tank, and headed for the beach. She quickly regretted not bringing a jacket and decided to jog to let out some frustration and stay warm at the same time.

The wind was strong, and the sky was gray and foggy. She suddenly had a longing for Colorado, a fire, and a hot cup of cocoa. She decided a hot bubble bath was probably better therapy than the beach tonight.

Once she had finished her bubble bath, she FaceTimed her grandchildren, which made the day worthwhile. She missed them so much, and it had been over three months since she had seen them. Her daughters were really her best friends, and the grandkids were growing so quickly. She knew she couldn't leave Brian until the end, and she really wanted to solve this mystery before he passed. But her soul was tired. She may need to ask for a four-day weekend to see her babies and recharge. She knew Marcy could use a break too and would talk to Brian and Marcy to see what they could schedule. She closed her eyes and was soon dreaming of laughing children.

She woke early and sensed a presence beside her. She slowly opened one eye and felt pressure on the bedside. It was dark, and she was unable to make out a face. She did not want to appear alarmed, but her adrenaline began pumping. "Marcy, is that you?" she whispered.

"No, love, it's Jack. I didn't want to wake you, but I found out some information. And I knew you got up early. I couldn't wait to share it with you."

"Jack, we need to set some boundaries. My bedroom is off-limits. You could have given me a heart attack, for cryin' out loud," she stated firmly, trying not to sound like a grouch but wanting him to know this behavior was not acceptable. She sat up and stretched. "What time is it anyway?"

"Almost five, what time do you normally get up?" He scooted up a little closer to the head of the bed but stayed on the edge.

"Between five and five thirty. What is so important that you had to barge in my room?" She reached over and turned on the light.

"I got a hit on that sketch. It belongs to a freelance photographer. He is actually doing a gig with *People* magazine right now, and they are sending me an update when they open. We are on the right track, Claire. I feel it in me bones."

"Sounds good. Actually, it sounds like the first bit of good news we have had in a while. Listen, Jack, I am happy, but I need to get up and moving. You need to go so I can do my morning routine. I will meet you downstairs in a bit."

"So you don't want the coffee I brought up for ya?" Jack smiled as he handed her a cup.

She had to admit that it smelled heavenly. "This doesn't smell like our coffee. Where did you find it?"

"It is from me own personal stash. I get it shipped from some mates in Costa Rica."

"Jack, do you realize that your accent changes when you are flirting versus when you are being professional?" She smiled.

"That's 'cuz I am more relaxed around you, lass. It should make you feel loved," he teased.

"Ha! Feel loved? You barely know me and trust me, there is a lot you don't know. I know you think you can smooth talk your way into a one-night stand, Jack Presley. But you need to know that I am not interested in the least. You can just back that train up all the way to the station and that includes coming into my bedroom without an invitation!"

His shoulders suddenly stiffened, and he stood up. "It's obvious you don't know me either, lassie. And I am getting a little miffed with everyone thinkin' I'm some kind a chancer. I'm not lookin' for a quick shag or snog, and you keep throwing it in my face. Keep in mind, you aren't the only one who grieves, missy. I have had my share of pain too. I'm not some himbo, and I don't appreciate being treated like one." He walked out the door and stomped down the hall.

Claire didn't understand half of what he had said but got the gist and actually felt bad for him. She hadn't meant to insult him. Truth was, she realized she had judged him without knowing anything about him. He had been very gentleman-like with her and didn't deserve to be scolded the way she did. Although she still did not appreciate him waltzing into her room unannounced. She jumped out of bed, got dressed as fast as she could, and went down to the kitchen to make some breakfast for them. She stopped quickly when she found him in the kitchen banging pans around and mumbling to himself.

"Look, Jack, you are absolutely right. I am sorry that I jumped to conclusions and judged you. I got defensive because I felt like you were moving a little too fast. But that didn't give me the right to jump all over you like that."

He was turned so that his back was facing her, and she couldn't see his face but saw his stance relax and could almost hear him smiling. "It's fine, love." He sighed. "Truth is, I probably was pushing too hard. I'm sorry too."

"Good. Let's make breakfast and talk about the case." She reached into the refrigerator and pulled out eggs and some vegetables.

"I'd rather talk about you. I know you just want friendship but even friends need to get to know each other." He grabbed some vegetables and started chopping.

She smiled to herself and felt heat in her cheeks. She was blushing and wasn't sure where to start. How do you sum up a lifetime of memories and lessons without revealing too much? "Well, I guess for starters, I have three daughters and six grandchildren. How about you? Any kids?"

"Nope, never did settle down long enough. I was married once about twenty years ago, but it didn't last long. And it actually kind of burned me on marriage." Somehow it was easier for them to talk while working and never really looking at each other.

"That bad, huh? It's never easy getting over a bad relationship. Of course, it isn't easy getting over a good one either. It took me a long time to let Dirk in after a bad divorce."

"Then you know what it's like. I haven't thought about her in a long time. I don't get angry anymore, though. She isn't worth it." She heard the sadness in his voice.

"Forgiveness is tough, Jack, but it works. When you carry a grudge, it only hurts yourself. Sounds like you have let it go and moved on."

"Aye, for the most part. I am sorry I never took the time to straddle down and have some kiddos, though. Would have been nice, I think."

"The best part of having kids is having grandchildren." She laughed. "It makes all the worst parts of parenthood worth it. Although I admit, once I got past the teenage years, my girls have become more like my best friends."

They worked in silence for a little while and became comfortable working side by side. They handed each other items without asking as if they had been making breakfast together for years. He told her stories about growing up in different countries and having to adjust.

He made another pot of his wonderful coffee and both were smiling and laughing by the time they sat to eat. "I will say this much for you, Jack. I am sure any woman would marry you in a heartbeat just to get this coffee," she teased.

"Ahh, good to know. So you're sayin' if I can't win them over with charm and good looks, then pull out the grounds?"

"I'm sure you don't have any problem with just the charm and looks, Jack."

"Well, you'd be wrong then, lass. Of course, I haven't tried very hard in quite a while."

They finished eating, and his phone rang. He smiled as he looked down and winked at her. "Just the news I was waiting for." He answered with, "What'd ya find out?"

She cleared the dishes and was loading the dishwasher when he came up behind her, picked her up, and spun around. She laughed and couldn't help but squeal. "Good news, I take it?"

"The best. Would you be willing to let me whisk you away to the Caicos?" He still had his arms wrapped around her.

"I can't, Jack. First of all, that would be pushing our friendship a little too fast for my taste. And most importantly, I can't leave Brian." She didn't want to offend him again, but she needed to be firm.

"I didn't figure ya could, but it couldn't hurt to ask," he replied sheepishly. "Good news, though, my source gave me a hit on the sketch, and he is in Caicos on an assignment. Not sure how long he will be there. So I am heading out as soon as I can nab a flight. You think I ought to give Brian the news or wait until I get more information?"

"If you don't mind, let me tell him as we go. I can judge his mood a little better, and I don't want to get his hopes up if this doesn't pan out."

"Good on ya then. I will call Mattie and give him the heads up. Better get to packin' then. Thank you for a wonderful breakfast and delicious company." He pulled her in for a hug, and she didn't resist. She had to admit to herself that it felt really good just to be hugged, and he smelled so good. She gently pulled away, and he lingered for a moment but turned and headed out the side door just as Marcy was coming down the stairs.

"Are you done with all your canoodling?" she teased.

Claire turned away, blushing. "I have no idea what you are talking about. I don't canoodle."

"Of course you do, and there is nothing wrong with it. Dirk has been gone awhile, and you aren't a nun," Marcy quipped.

"I am not ready for a relationship especially the kind Jack is used to. I have been perfectly happy on my own and don't need any other distractions besides my family, friends, and work. Besides, he is leaving today on a lead. Who knows if and when he will be back." Claire couldn't hide a hint of disappointment in her voice.

"Oh by golly, he'll be back. You might not be interested in him which I think is hogwash but he is sure all googly-eyed over you. I don't reckon he is a man that gives up that easily."

"I need to go check on Brian. He isn't eating or drinking much and sleeping a lot. Every time he goes out for an outing anymore, it completely wipes him out. I am really concerned that his time may be getting close." Claire headed toward the backroom as Gerard was coming down the hall, still in his pajamas, yawning and rubbing his eyes.

"Good morning, Ms. Claire." He yawned. "Mr. Montgomery had a rough night. I think he is having nightmares."

"Why didn't you come get me, Gerard? I would have been happy to stay with him."

"I would have if I really thought you could do anything, but I think he just needed someone there if he woke up. He didn't seem like he was in pain, and I am a lot closer. It is fine, really. I don't mind."

"Okay, but that is why I am here. Next time, come get me or just send me a text to come down. You and Sable have enough on your plate. Please let Marcy help you with some household chores today." Claire gave him a quick hug and headed towards Brian's room.

Brian was sleeping when she walked in, but she could see that he was restless. She went over to the cabinet to get his morning medications ready. She took his vital signs and was not pleased. His blood pressure was very low, his pulse was very high, and he was sweating profusely. She hummed softly as she administered his liquid medication. His breathing slowed a little, and he became less fidgety. She had been a hospice nurse long enough to know that his time was becoming shorter by the day. She placed some cool rags on his forehead and pulled up the rocking chair and TV tray so that she could stay beside him and work on the computer. She sent an email update to Matthew. Normally she kept in close touch with family members who were out of town and became really sad when she thought about Brian not having any family or people close who cared enough to get an update. Once again, she was so grateful for Gerard, Sable, and other staff members here. They had become Brian's family, and from what she could tell, they were just as worried about him and cared for him as much, if not more, than many family members she had dealt with in the past.

Jack poked his head in an hour later and let her know that Matthew had sent a plane, and he would be leaving. He kissed her on the forehead and promised to stay in touch. In some ways, she was relieved that he wouldn't be here for a while, yet she knew she would miss him. She really didn't know what to think or feel when it came to Jack Presley.

"Claire," Brian croaked, "can I have some water?"

Claire fixed him a glass, adjusted the bed, and helped him take a few sips. "I saw my mother last night. Is that normal?"

"Sometimes. Remember, I told you that every journey is different. But yes, some people see others that have passed before them. Are you afraid?" She kept her voice as comforting as she could and stroked his forehead.

"No, it wasn't as if she was dead. I saw her holding me as a child. I was crying, and she was trying to comfort me."

"You haven't talked much about your family, Brian. Do you want to?"

"Not much to talk about, really. My mother was an alcoholic and popped pills. She died when I was a teenager, and there have been claims about half-brothers and sisters from my father's side, but only one agreed to a paternity test. She was supposedly a user too and stopped coming after me when I stopped sending money. I have no idea where she is now. The other is supposedly a brother that looked enough like me to pass. He was a drug dealer, mine for a while actually. Anyway, he ended up in prison, and I haven't heard from him in a long time. Obviously addiction runs rampant in my family genes, and maybe that is partially why I never wanted children. I have been on my own for a long time. Not used to having people close to me, you know?"

Claire could tell that it was difficult for him to talk. His breathing was ragged, and he seemed to have problems struggling with words. Tank waddled into the room and sat between her and Brian who reached down and pet his head. Brian eventually drifted back to sleep, and Tank parked himself right by the bed and plopped down. She felt a vibration from her phone and noticed it was Matthew calling. She answered softly and stepped out of the room, closing the door behind her.

Matthew had gotten the update on Brian's condition and was calling to check in. He told Claire that he no longer felt comfortable leaving the matter in their own hands and had contacted the chief of police to let him know what was going on. The chief was willing to let them continue their investigation and didn't seem to be in a huge rush to arrest and prosecute a dying man. Matthew stated the chief wasn't very happy about the situation though and wanted to talk to Brian when it was feasible. Matthew wanted to let Claire know that he would be sending a copy of all the information they had so far along with all of Jack's notes to the chief in an overnight package. He told Claire to expect a call or visit in the next few days. Matthew was hoping Jack would have more information to add before that happened.

"Even if we solve this mystery before he dies, I am not sure he is able to comprehend anything right now, Matthew." Claire felt discouraged.

"Well, that is something we can pray for together then. I can't tell you how grateful I am to have you and Marcy there for him right now. You both are just what he needed."

"Thank you for that. I'm sure Marcy would be grateful to hear it from you as well. Any idea when you might be back?"

"Whisper and I will be flying down this weekend. Do me a favor and don't tell Marcy, though. I would like to surprise her."

"That's wonderful! Marcy will be so excited to see her! Oh, thank you, dear. You just made my day."

"Well, don't look too happy. We don't want Marcy to get suspicious." He chuckled.

After they hung up, Claire went to find Sable and let her in on the secret so they could prepare rooms for Matthew and Whisper. She found two of John's children in the kitchen, making cookies with Sable and Marcy. She stopped in the hallway to eavesdrop and admire the scene. She longed for her own grandchildren but knew the timing would not be right for her to leave right now. John's youngest, the one with Down syndrome, was humming a tune she had never heard before.

"Wow, looks like you guys are having fun. What is that tune you are humming? It sounds lovely," Claire asked as she came into the room.

"It's a Brazilian song my mamma taught me. In Portuguese, it means a pretty young rose," the boy boasted.

"It's beautiful, Jake. Can you sing it for me?" Claire smiled. The boy struggled with some of the Portuguese, but his sister chimed in and helped him.

They did a beautiful job, and everyone clapped when they finished. Jasmine, his sister, blushed when Claire told her how lovely her voice was. Jasmine offered Claire one of the cookies and blushed even more when Claire gushed at how delicious they were. Claire suggested the kids take some out to their fathers Ernesto and Manuel.

"They are such good kids," Marcy said as they left. "That Jasmine is going to be a heartbreaker just like my Whisper was at that age. Dagnabit, I need grandkids! I'm not getting any younger!"

"You still have two daughters. It isn't their fault that they are both beautiful and independent," Claire chided.

"Sunshine has already told me she doesn't want children. She loves the travel that her job offers and doesn't want to settle down.

Plus she has already hit her prime childbearing years and never had the biological clock tick at her. Whisper, well, I don't know what is going on in that brain of hers, but she is definitely a workaholic and loves that office. Truth be told, I am not so sure she has a love life, she never wants to talk about it." Marcy looked a little dejected. "Timber was my true hope for grandbabies with all his charm and cattin' around. Lordy above, I miss that boy."

Claire reached over to give her friend a hug. She couldn't imagine what it would be like to lose a child, that constant pain that grieving never relieves. Marcy allowed to be just held for a moment, then cleared her throat and busied herself. The two worked in silence for a few moments before Claire remembered why she had come in.

"Do you know where Sable is? I would like to talk to her and Gerard about revamping the library a little more since I have a feeling one of us will be spending more time in there.

"She and Gerry are out shopping. Let me finish up in here then I will come help." Marcy's voice still carried so much sadness.

"You know what? Why don't you and Ernesto go out to the town tonight?" Claire suggested. "I think you could use some time away from here, and you haven't left the compound for a while just to have fun.

"I don't know... I am not even sure Ernesto is interested anymore. I think I pushed the whole "hard to get" envelope a little too far."

"Well, how about if I pretend I am more like you and become more pushy at the matchmaking." Claire was out the door before Marcy could protest. While she was out, she called Sable and let her and Gerard in on the secret so they could pick up any extra supplies they might need. She found Ernesto in the garden, barking orders at Manuel who was enjoying a cookie and the break with the children.

Claire began picking weeds with Ernesto, who softened slightly with her presence. "Ma'am, do you need chives for a meal?"

"No, at least, I don't think so. Why?"

"Because that is what you are pulling and not very well, I must say." Ernesto couldn't hide the frustration in his voice.

"Oh, I am sorry." She dropped what she thought were weeds and brushed her hands on her pants. "I suppose it isn't much help if I don't know what I am doing. I am sorry, Ernesto. I should have left this to the expert. I was only trying to help and get a moment to speak with you." Claire was truly embarrassed.

"It's okay, ma'am, but you are not helping, so please don't touch the garden. What would you need to speak to me about?" Ernesto gently pushed her aside while trying to fix the soil where she had ripped up the plants.

"I just thought that maybe you and Marcy could go out tonight for some dinner and dancing. I know she could use some time away, and I thought it would be good for you also," Claire mumbled; she wasn't used to being so forward.

"I don't think Ms. Marcy likes me much. I think I am not good enough for her. She always leaves when I come close to her. I am not sure if I have offended her in some way." Ernesto would not look at Claire, but she could hear the discouragement in his voice.

"No, no, Ernesto. She does like you, but it has been a long time since anyone has shown interest in her. So she doesn't quite know what to do with her feelings. I am afraid some of that might be my fault. Since my husband died, Marcy has always been available to me for traveling, dinners, movies… I am afraid I have completely intruded on her having any kind of relationship away from our friendship. Plus we are at that age where we are not interested in the same types of relationships we had when we were younger and dating. Does that make sense?"

"Yes, ma'am, but why she runs away all the time?" Ernesto was struggling with his English and looked like a puppy who had just been scolded.

"Oh, Ernesto, I wish I could tell you what goes on in that woman's head at times. But I know that she is also trying to honor God in her relationships and might be a little afraid of getting too close."

"She wants to be nun then? I think she is too pretty to be nun." Ernesto was shaking his head and running his hands through his thick, wavy gray hair.

"No, no. She just doesn't want to get too close to anyone before marriage. She doesn't want to make any mistakes… she doesn't…"

Ernesto gave her puzzling looks, then it suddenly dawned on him what she was trying to say. He made the crucifix sign across his chest and began speaking Spanish at lightning speed.

"Slow down, Ernesto, my Spanish is not very good," Claire begged, almost laughing.

"I am offended that you could think I am that type of man, Ms. Claire. I never thought of mi amor in such a way. I wish to broom her off her feet."

Claire did laugh at that point. "I think you meant 'sweep her off her feet.' I know you would never intentionally hurt her, Ernesto. I didn't mean to offend you either, and I am truly sorry if I did. How about if you take her out and let her know how you feel. In my experience, communication is the most important part of developing a romance. I think you should let her know your frustration. I will even make the reservation and pay for it."

Ernesto stiffened. "Now you don't think I can pay my own way? Aye, yai, yai…" Ernesto slammed the shovel into the soft dirt.

"No! Oh my, Ernesto! I am so sorry! Please, I am not very good at this! This is Marcy's forte, not mine. Please don't let my fumbling attempts offend you any more than they already have!" Claire was almost in tears, thinking that she had hurt the sweet man's feelings.

Thankfully, Manuel who had been listening the whole time stepped in and spoke to Ernesto in Spanish. Ernesto glared at Claire, shaking his head. Claire was beside herself wringing her hands, wishing she had learned more than the basic medical Spanish. She could only pick out a few words, but she got the impression that Manuel was doing a much better job at explaining her motives.

Manuel tried to keep from laughing and looked at Claire throughout the discussion smiling and offering a wink. Finally Ernesto came and extended his hand to Claire. "*Gracias*, Ms. Claire for trying to help. You do make me feel better about my feelings for Ms. Marcy. I thought she no like me anymore. I will go ask her for a proper date, yes?"

Claire was relieved and reached over to hug him. "Yes! Oh, Ernesto, that would be wonderful. *Gracias, mi amigo!*"

Once he had left for the main house, Claire grabbed Manuel and hugged him tightly. "I am not sure what you said, but thank you so much for interceding on my behalf. I made a fool of myself."

"It's okay, Ms. Claire, but you should know that my uncle is what you would call a man's man and doesn't really communicate well on his own either. He has a lot of stubborn pride, and it has been many years since he has tried his hand at trying to romance a woman. He isn't very good at it." Manuel was chuckling. "I should have stepped in sooner, but you two were my entertainment for the afternoon. You can actually dig a pretty good hole yourself, Ms. Claire."

Manuel smiled and offered a hug back. He offered her some words in Spanish that she could use to talk to Ernesto a little better and advised her what area of the garden to stay away from.

They both turned back and saw Ernesto actually kick his heels in the air as he came running out of the main house.

"She must have said yes." Claire laughed and gave Manuel a high-five.

Claire found Marcy in the kitchen, scrubbing furiously when she came back in. "I take it you said yes to Ernesto to go out tonight?"

"Yeah, but now I am regretting it. I didn't pack anything to go out on a date with, and I only have my comfy clothes here. I have no idea what I am going to wear, I haven't had my nails or hair done in months… I look like a haggard old mess."

"How about if you and I pull a *Pretty Woman*? We can go shopping, hit the nail and hair salon together? I haven't been out in a long time either except for the yacht trips, and that wasn't really helpful. I will go check on Brian and see if Isabelle can sit with him until Sable and Gerard get back. Come on, it will do us both some good, and I am buying. No arguments."

Marcy stopped scrubbing and looked at Claire. "Do you really mean it? That would be the bomb!" Marcy danced around in a circle and giggled. "Yippee! Look out, world. We are about to bedazzle ya!"

Claire adjusted Brian and gave him medication. She was still very worried about leaving him, but he looked comfortable and didn't even open his eyes while she provided care for him. She cleaned him, changed his sheets, and left a list for Isabelle of signs to look for and call her if needed. She expected Sable and Gerard back within an hour or two and felt safe leaving Brian in Isabelle's care until then.

She jumped in the shower and thought about Jack for the first time that day. She hated to admit it, but there was a small part of her that was a little jealous that Marcy and Ernesto were going out on a date. It would have been nice to get all dolled up for a date herself. She quickly shook those feelings away and was looking forward to seeing Marcy back to her bubbly self.

Claire felt good about her decision as Marcy hummed and jabbered all the way into town. They went to the nail salon first, and Marcy talked Claire into some airbrushed nail art. Marcy took a little longer at the beauty shop since Claire just wanted a trim and didn't need the full blown styling. While she was waiting, Claire decided to run over to the coffee shop and get them a Chai Tea. Her phone rang while she was walking back, and she struggled to get it out of her purse with her hands full.

When she finally reached it, she realized she missed the call but didn't recognize the number and was hesitant to return the call. She called Gerard to check on Brian and asked him if he recognized the number. He didn't, but he did say that Jack had called the house looking for her. When she hung up with Gerard, she paused a minute before returning the initial call.

"Nope, not gonna call. This is Marcy's day. Brian is fine, and everyone else can wait," Claire told herself as she shoved the phone back into her purse.

The girls found an upscale boutique, and Marcy had chosen a beautiful red silk and chiffon blouse with black palazzo pants and rhinestoned red flats. Claire would never admit to Marcy, but she was a little concerned that the outfit was a bit classier than Ernesto was planning. But Marcy glowed and looked beautiful, so Claire kept her skepticism to herself. They stopped at the market to grab a home dry-cleaning packet since they didn't have time to actually have the outfit properly. Claire drove as Marcy gushed about how wonderful the day was and thanked Claire profusely all the way back. Marcy went through the front door and straight up the stairs, not wanting anyone to see her until she was ready. Marcy felt like the queen of the ball as she busied herself, getting ready for her date.

Ernesto, being the gentleman that he was, rang the main doorbell at precisely 7:00 p.m. Claire told Sable this was how it felt when she was getting her girls ready for prom night. Ernesto looked dashing in a black suit and had a dozen long-stemmed red roses ready and waiting for his lady. Marcy looked a little nervous as she descended, but her eyes twinkled and everyone laughed as she let out a whistle when she saw Ernesto at the bottom of the stairs. Ernesto grabbed her hand and kissed her knuckles, saying something softly in Spanish that made Marcy blush.

"I have no idea what you said, darling but say it again, you just made my heart melt a little," she said to Ernesto as she reached over to kiss his cheek. She handed the roses to Gerard. "Make sure you treat these with kid gloves, I have saved every flower Ernie has given me."

The pair looked like two teenagers totally smitten with each other. Marcy winked at Claire, Sable, and Gerard. "Don't wait up, loves. I don't plan on returning anytime soon."

"Oh, let me snap a picture first. You both look so glamorous, and I am sure Whisper and Sunshine would love to see it." Claire took the picture and hugged both before they left. The three remaining walked back to the kitchen and sat down to a light salad and glass of wine. They toasted each other for Marcy and Ernesto, and Gerard gave a touching toast to his own bride. Claire couldn't help but feel a little lonely as Sable and Gerard gazed lovingly at each other.

"Tell us a little about Marcy's daughter." Sable sensed Claire's uneasiness. "Is she as spunky as Marcy?"

Claire relaxed and told stories of when both of their children were young. "She is smart and has Marcy's flair for style but is much more professional and toned down than her mother. You will love her."

Claire helped with the cleanup and headed back to Brian's room. Gerard had offered to stay with him tonight, but Claire knew she would feel better if she did it herself. She sent a quick text to Manuel to thank him for helping get Ernesto ready and sent another to Isabelle, thanking her for her help that afternoon. She called each of the kids, but everyone was busy, so she kept the conversations short. She sat staring at her phone, trying to talk herself into calling Jack. When the phone rang, she jumped.

"Hello? Claire?" the connection was bad, but she recognized his voice, and a warm feeling washed over her.

"Jack, it's me. Can you hear me?"

"Not well, love. Let me ring you on the hotel line."

She waited five minutes before he called back, but she could hear him crystal clear.

"Ah, much better. I tried ringing you earlier but you must have been busy." Claire curled up in a chair and told him about the day. Jack asked all kinds of questions about Ernesto since he hadn't really gotten to know him well in the short time Jack was at the compound. "Sounds like a lucky bloke, I must admit, I'm a little jealous."

"Why's that?" Claire asked. "Were you hoping to broom Marcy off her feet too?" Claire laughed.

Jack chuckled. "I think you are well aware of whom I want to broom. I'm a little jealous, I couldn't be there to woo you, my love."

"Well, I am sure there are plenty of beauties on that island, Mr. Presley. You should be out slathering your charm on some of them." Claire teased.

"Not likely, lass. You aren't about to blow me off that quick, are ya?" Jack sounded teasing and hesitant at the same time.

"I guess I could give a lad a chance… maybe. I don't really know to be honest with you. Oh, let's change the subject. How was your day?"

Jack told her about his lead on the bearded man from the sketch. He tracked the man to a nearby hotel, but the concierge had told them that he checked out the day before. Jack did manage to get a name and was still looking to see if he was on the island. "I've given his name to Mattie. And I don't know how to explain it, but I have a feeling in me bones that the maggot is still here."

"Come on now, Jack, you can't be sure he is a… maggot. He may be innocent in all this." Claire wanted to be objective and not jump to conclusions. She was just hoping this mystery man might be able to lead them in the right direction. "Have you heard anything back from Matthew on where Peter is yet?"

"I've got a hunch, but I don't want to divulge anything too soon. I have a meet with a source in the morning."

"That's good. I am sure you have been doing this long enough that your instincts are usually right," Claire said.

"With the job, yes, I trust my instincts. With you, I'm not so sure. I haven't been able to get you off my mind, Claire."

They were both silent for a minute before Claire spoke up. "I have to admit, I thought of you today too. I am just very hesitant, Jack. I want to get to know you better, but I just don't think I am ready for a relationship of any kind. I don't want to lead you on, but I can't make any promises right now."

"It's okay, love. I can be patient sometimes. I realize it is not my strong suit, but I have a feeling you are worth the wait."

"Thank you, Jack. I need to look after Brian now, so I'm going to let you go." Claire knew that Brian didn't need anything but was unsure of where the conversation was leading.

"Nonsense, I know you well enough to know that you are in the room with him now, and he is probably sound asleep. If you don't want to talk to me anymore, just say so. I promise I won't play games with you, Claire. But you need to promise the same."

Claire sighed. "Okay, I promise. Tell me more about your relationship with Matthew."

Jack laughed. "Chicken." But he relaxed and began telling her stories of some of the cases Matthew had him work on. Claire felt much more secure talking to him about his past. They laughed and talked for an hour before Brian started to stir.

"Okay, not lying. I really do have to take care of Brian now," Claire interrupted. "This has been lovely, Jack. Thank you for a wonderful evening."

"My pleasure, love. Dream of me, will you?" Jack hung up before she could respond.

chapter
9

It was eleven o'clock the next morning before Marcy came down from her room. She literally glided down the backstairs and hummed as she put on a pot of coffee. Sable and Claire looked at each other, smiling. "I take it the date went well?" Claire asked.

"Better than I could ever imagine, and you know how good my imagination is, sugarplum," Marcy sang.

"Are you going to tell us about it?" Sable teased. "Or just let our imaginations run wild?"

"He was a perfect gentleman. We talked and danced, then ate and talked, then talked and danced… we walked and danced down by the ocean. It was heavenly."

"Did you let him kiss you?" Claire asked.

"Of course I did. Actually he was unsure if he should, so I kissed him first. There was a lot of kissing after that, but don't you worry, Ms. Nosey. Nothing else happened as far as that is concerned. I was a good girl. The Lord had to help, but I curbed myself pretty well."

"Good for you. It warms my bones to see you so happy." Claire's smile was just as brilliant as Marcy's. Claire sent a silent prayer up that Ernesto was really as wonderful as Marcy had hoped. Marcy had been burned in the past pretty badly with one man leaving her and her bank account almost empty.

Claire heard Brian moaning on the monitor which broke the smiles, and the ladies stared at the small screen with concerned looks.

"Wow, he looks so different than that Greek God I saw naked in the garden the first day we were here." Marcy noted. "How did that happen so fast?" She asked Claire.

"Cancer does that. It steals muscle, and patients literally waste away little by little. I need to position him differently. Sable, can you ask Gerard to come help me in a few minutes? I am going to clean him up a little first but will need help. I would also like to change his sheets and freshen up the room today as well."

"Should I fix him a smoothie? I know he didn't like them at first, but he has liked the last few I have given him." Marcy wanted so badly to cure him with her concoctions.

"Sure, it can't hurt. But he really hasn't wanted to eat or drink much in the last few days, so don't be disappointed if it sits untouched." Claire gathered some supplies and turned off the monitor when she entered the room.

Claire took her time cleaning him, she talked to him constantly when she was in the room. She knew from experience that even when patients are unable to respond, hearing is the last sense to go.

"I talked to Jack last night, you know. He has a lead to check out this morning. I sincerely pray you can hold on until we figure this mess out so you can truly go in peace. Matthew and Whisper are coming tomorrow. Feel like waking up so you can finally meet Whisper? I know she would love to meet you. You two have worked together for so long, and even though your face is famous, she hasn't really gotten to know the Brian that we know. I need to check your skin so don't squirm. I realize this is not your favorite part of my job, but it is essential. I won't have you developing any skin ulcers just because you are prideful." She performed a full examination and was humming softly when Brian opened his eyes and gave her a glaring look.

She smiled. "Don't look at me like that, mister. You know I have to do this."

"I know but do you have to talk incessantly?" His voice was weak and hoarse. "Can't Gerard do this?"

"Brian, this is my job. I know it makes you uncomfortable, but I have been doing this for a very long time and trust me, nothing you have or do is new to me. I would think that by now, you could trust me. I make sure the monitor is off, and only Gerard and I take care of your intimate needs." She tried to be as reassuring as possible.

"I know, I know, but I still feel strange." His voice was hoarse and barely a whisper. "Did I hear you say Matthew is coming?"

"Yes, he should be here tomorrow. He sounded excited about something, and he is bringing Whisper with him. Won't it be nice to finally meet her?"

"It will. I feel like I know her so well already. And after getting to know Marcy, I feel even closer to her. I am sure she knows everything that is going on, but I still feel leery that so many people know about the boat. How long before we have to involve the police?"

"Actually Matthew already told the police. He notified the commissioner himself a few days ago. They have called a few times, and we have given them all the information we have. But Matthew asked if he and Jack can be the go-between because of your condition."

They heard a knock on the door, and Gerard slipped in. Both Claire and Gerard finished cleaning him, changing sheets, and decided it would be good for Brian to sit in the chair for a while. They exchanged worried glances when they were transferring him to the chair. Brian was a lot weaker than he was even a few days ago.

"Stop fretting, you two, I can feel the tension in here. I am okay with dying. I have had a lot of time in the last month to really review my life, and it wasn't so bad." Both Claire and Gerard sat in front of him silently. "I want to get this mess straightened out but even if I don't before I die, I trust you all to fix it. I just don't want the press to get wind of it and tarnish every good thing I have done in my life. I don't want a scandal to be my legacy."

"I can guarantee you that your legacy is safe, sir. Even if it takes until my last breath and last penny, I will make sure this story remains safely tucked." Gerard had difficulty not shedding tears.

"There is a reason I put you in charge, brother." Brian wiggled into the chair and closed his eyes. Marcy breezed into the room a few minutes later with a frosted glass in hand and laughed when Brian winced. He sat up a little straighter and took a sip.

"Not bad, hippie, not bad." He smiled and winked at Marcy.

"I am getting better at customizing them to your taste." Marcy began fluffing pillows behind him.

"So, hippie, you are positively glowing today. If you weren't so old, I would say you were pregnant. Did you get lucky without me?" Brian teased.

Marcy promptly hit him in the head with a pillow. "None of your beeswax, buster!"

"Ah. That means yes. Who is the poor schmuck that fell victim to your womanly wiles?"

Claire and Gerard chuckled and let Marcy have some time rehashing her date. Gerard spotted Claire checking her cell phone for the fifth time in thirty minutes and asked her about it as they headed for his office.

"I thought Jack would have called by now. He had a meeting with a source this morning and promised to get back with me as soon as he had some information."

"I am sure he will call you soon. Do you have any idea why Matthew and Whisper are coming?"

"Not really. Matthew was very vague but wanted to make sure that Marcy was surprised. Maybe it is as simple as letting Marcy and Whisper see each other."

"I am sure she will be. I have Sable preparing the main dining room for dinner. Thankfully Marcy doesn't go in there often."

"Why is she preparing the dining room today? They won't be here until tomorrow," Claire asked.

"Oh no, ma'am. He called this morning and said they would be here this afternoon. He was able to rearrange his schedule. He actually sounded excited."

"I will be happy to see them, but I can't help wondering about the change of plans. Do you think it has anything to do with the case?"

Gerard shook his head. "I was hoping you would know more, Ms. Claire."

"Well, regardless, let's go get things ready. I will tell Manuel and Ernesto take the car over to the airport for them."

"I am one step ahead of you, ma'am. They left before I came in to help with Mr. Montgomery."

"Oh darn, I must confess, I wanted to see if Ernesto was as giddy as Marcy was this morning about their date." Claire giggled.

"They should be back soon, but I can assure you, Ernesto was beaming when I saw him."

"Should we send Marcy on an errand so that she can't see them pull up? Do we have an idea of arrival time?"

"All I know, ma'am, is that we should expect them for dinner. I can ask Marcy if she would like to go down to the market with me for some fresh shrimp."

"That might work. Would you like for me to help get the guest cottage cleaned up?"

"No, ma'am. Isabelle cleaned it after Mr. Jack left. So there isn't much to do. I will prepare a room for Matthew. I will have Isabelle run over some of Marcy's things to the guesthouse so that she can spend some time with her daughter."

"How would this place ever survive without you, Gerard?"

"I hope we never have to find out, ma'am," he said softly.

chapter 10

Marcy spent a few hours with Brian reading the latest Hollywood rags and playing cards. She turned down Gerard's offer to run into town, so Claire asked Ernesto if he wouldn't mind taking her for a walk by the beach; and of course, he was very willing to sneak off with her alone for some time. Claire couldn't help but smile as she watched the two walk hand in hand towards the path. It seemed as if they had each taken years off their age, and their steps were much lighter overnight. Marcy was a little suspicious when Claire asked her to take her phone with her, but Claire easily explained it as concern ever since her encounter with Peter.

Claire glanced at her own phone for what felt like the millionth time that day, wondering if she should call Jack but deciding it would be better to wait. He promised he would call if the lead turned into anything valuable, so she should trust that, but patience was never her strongest virtue.

She and Gerard were helping Sable with dinner when they heard the front door open. Matthew peeked his head in the kitchen. "Is it safe to come in?"

Claire laughed and hugged both of them tightly. "Let's go put your things away, and I will have you wait in the dining room while I call Marcy. She is going to flip!"

"I can't wait to see her. It has been a long time since we have gone so long without seeing each other," Whisper smiled.

"I can relate. Honestly I can't wait to get back to Colorado to see the girls. It feels like it has been a year even though it's only been a few months." Claire hugged her again. "You look positively radiant, Whisper. I can't wait to see your mom's face when she sees you."

Claire called Marcy while the kids were getting settled and had to laugh when it took longer than she thought to talk Marcy into coming back.

Marcy and Ernesto did not look happy when they walked into the dining room, but half of Florida could hear her scream when she saw her daughter. "You're gonna be the death of me, child! Lordy it is good to see your face!"

Marcy and Whisper hugged, laughed, and danced around for several minutes as if no one was in the room. Matthew stood back smiling, and Claire knew immediately the reason for the visit. Matthew and Whisper were in love.

Claire cleared her throat as Gerard wheeled Brian into the room. Matthew tore his gaze away to greet his client and friend. Marcy and Whisper, still arm in arm, smiled and made introductions.

"Matthew, you son of a gun. Why didn't you tell me you stole the most beautiful woman for yourself?" Brian teased.

Matthew's cheeks were bright red, but he lightly punched Brian on the shoulder. "Couldn't let her meet you until I was sure she wouldn't run off with you."

Marcy was stunned as she looked from Whisper to Matthew and back to Whisper. "Good Lord, I think I am going to have a heart attack. How could you not tell me? How long has this been going on? Is this a joke, are you kidding me?"

Matthew came over to Marcy. "Blame me, not Whisper. I asked her to keep our relationship between us since we work so closely together, and I didn't want to start rumors. I am truly sorry we didn't tell you sooner. If it makes you feel any better, it was very hard for Whisper not to tell you."

"Come on, Matt. You know that's not true. Mom, I love you with all my heart, but you can't keep a secret for anything. Plus I wasn't sure I could answer the barrage of questions and the continual nagging about a wedding date and when we would have kids." Whisper laughed.

"So when is the wedding date, and when can I expect a grand-child?" Marcy laughed as she held Whisper's face in her hands lovingly.

"How about seven months from now?" Whisper smiled.

Marcy was speechless as she sat down, clearly in shock. "You are joking, right?" Marcy said seriously.

The others in the room looked at Matthew and seemed a little uncomfortable witnessing their exchange.

Matthew walked up behind Marcy and placed his hand on her shoulder. "No joking here, Mom."

Marcy glared at Matthew. "I realize, young man, that I may seem very free-spirited to you, but I am having a difficult time being excited and disappointed all at once." She turned and looked at Whisper. "This isn't how it is supposed to work. You are supposed to get married first. I love you, and I will love this child, but this is so much all at once."

"It's okay, Mom, I know this is crazy. Matthew and I didn't mean to pile all of this on you at once. How about if we sit and can tell you the story?"

Gerard, Sable, and Claire took that as a cue to bring in dinner. Ernesto stood in the doorway, not knowing if he should stay or leave. He had never eaten in the main dining room with Mr. Montgomery and felt very out of place, but he didn't want to leave Marcy if she was distraught in any way. Luckily Claire noticed his discomfort and guided him to the chair next to Marcy. He glanced at Brian, who smiled and nodded and indicated for him to sit and join them.

Marcy felt Ernesto slip his arm around her shoulders and leaned into him grabbing his hand. Whisper gave her mother a puzzling look and said, "Looks like I am not the only one keeping secrets. Something you want to tell me, Mom?"

Marcy smiled and looked back at Ernesto. "Mine hasn't been a secret for long, and you would have known by the weekend, missy, so don't think you can get out of this one so easy. Whisper, meet Ernie, this is the man I told you about last time we talked."

Ernesto stood to shake Whisper's hand, but she grabbed both hands and hugged him warmly. "Mom has told me so much about you. It is a pleasure to meet you. I didn't think you two were actually an item yet though, although I knew Mom was definitely smitten with you."

"Brian, I don't want to be disrespectful, but is it all right if I say a prayer before we eat? We have so much to be thankful for," Claire asked.

Brian shrugged his shoulders. "It's fine," he said softly and even bowed his head and closed his eyes as they offered the blessing. Dinner was spirited with questions, laughing, teasing, and learning that Matthew and Whisper had actually been dating for over a year.

"Do you remember when Brian called me a couple of weeks ago?" Matthew asked Marcy who nodded. "Well, I wasn't lying when I said I was in France, but what I didn't tell you is why. We were actually on our honeymoon."

"What? Why didn't you tell me then?" Marcy asked, a little hurt.

"Because we knew how you felt about my getting pregnant before we were married. I was ashamed, Mom." Whisper bowed her head.

"This is the twenty-first century, Whisper," Brian said tersely. "You have nothing to be ashamed about."

"It's okay, Brian," Matthew said. "Actually I was embarrassed and wanted to ask your blessing, Marcy, but Whisper didn't want to tell you until she could tell you in person and let you know that we were married. I offered to bring her with me then, but she had a lot of morning sickness and didn't think she should make the fast trip back. Plus I wanted to give Brian my undivided attention, considering his situation."

"That doesn't make all of this okay," Marcy said, "but I do understand the secrecy a little more."

Brian was clearly irritated. "Well, I for one don't give a damn if they were married first, so I will raise a toast to my friend." He lifted his glass. "To the happy couple." He took a drink and slammed his glass on the table.

"I think I will retire to my room before all the Jesus freaks start ruining the happy moment."

Gerard stood hesitantly and stood behind the wheelchair. "Mattie boy, if you need a stiff drink after they all grill you to death, you know where to find me. Whisper, I wish I had met you sooner and made you doubt our boy here, but I wish you the best. Take care of Mattie, I know you will. Goodnight all."

Marcy looked at Whisper. "You know the worst part of this? I have been planning your wedding since you were three years old, and now I can't give it to you."

"Oh, Mom, I love you so much, but your wedding plans were never my dream. How about if we compromise, and you can throw us a big reception when you get home? I can show you the video of our ceremony. I know it isn't the same, but you can see that we had a chair for you, Dad, Timber, and Matthew's parents."

"But I am not dead yet! And what about Sunshine? Don't you think she would have liked to be a part of your day?"

"She was, Mom, she was my maid of honor." Whisper sounded sad.

"So am I the only one who was excluded?" Marcy cried. "This is not making me feel better."

"Look, Mom, I never planned to exclude you. I promise. I understand you are hurt, and I am so sorry. That was never my intent."

They all sat silent for a while when Claire's phone rang and startled them all a little. She excused herself, and both Sable and Ernesto began to pick up dishes. It was clear that Marcy, Whisper, and Matthew needed time alone to talk alone.

Once everyone was gone, Whisper attempted to make a truce. "How about if we have a small ceremony or reception while we are here? Would that help?"

Marcy smiled at the genuine attempt. "No, dear, it's fine. Honestly I am relieved not to have to pay for the wedding of my… I mean your dreams. I am happy for you, truly I am. I just wish the timeline would have been a little different. I don't even know how you feel about your spirituality Matthew. For me, that is much more important. So talk to me. Let me know how and where each of you are. It would break my heart if my grandchild was raised without knowing the Lord."

Whisper blushed. "We don't want that either, Mom. I know that our timeline isn't perfect, and both of us are truly sorry, not just to you but to God as well. I could try and justify our sin by saying that we were never intimate until after Matthew proposed, but I know it was a sin regardless."

Matthew came behind Whisper and placed his hand on her shoulder. "You know, I think the ceremony formalized our union, but I have felt married to Whisper for much longer. I adore your daughter and only want to make her happy for as long as we are on this earth. I have never considered myself religious, but I am spiritual, and I have always thought that was enough. I realize that Whisper grew up in a church environment, but my family was more of a Buddhist philosophy, I guess. It wasn't until Whisper and I started doing a Bible study that I even discovered the love and sacrifice that Christ offered. It is because of your daughter that I was saved. And just so you know, she told me later that if I hadn't accepted Christ as my Savior, she would not have agreed to marry me. She didn't want to make it an ultimatum, but she is firm in her belief and it was that important to her."

"Oh, Matthew, thank you! You have no idea how happy that makes me," Marcy cried. "Let's go for a walk and talk some more. I have missed you, baby girl." She hugged Whisper tightly, and both cried in each other's arms.

"If it is all right with you, ladies, I am going to talk to Brian while you two catch up. I would like to go over some business with him." Matthew felt it was important for his new wife to get some closure. Her anxiety about telling Marcy everything was causing her so much stress lately. He sent up a silent prayer of thanks that it turned out better than she had anticipated.

Matthew knocked on the library door and found Brian sitting in his wheelchair, staring out the window.

"How come you never told me about this romance? I have always thought of you as a friend." Brian asked.

"I think of you as a friend, too, Monty. But I have always had to keep secrets for my clients, and I guess I am just not used to telling anyone anything either personally or professionally. Do you have a problem with it?"

"No, man, I am happy for you but do you buy into all their religious mumbo jumbo? I can't believe they made such a big deal about her being pregnant before you two got hitched. What business is it of theirs? It makes me so angry that Marcy was rude to you just because you didn't live up to her perfect standards."

"I didn't see it that way at all. Marcy only wants what is best for her daughter. I may not have understood until faced with fatherhood myself, but I understand her reaction. And yeah, I buy into a God who loves me and is willing to forgive if I mess up and admit it. Just like Marcy and Whisper have made up and are out catching up now, forgiveness comes a lot easier when someone understands the true sacrifice Christ made for all of us."

"Sorry to disappoint you, dude, I just don't get it." Brian sounded sad.

"How about if we change the subject?" Matthew pulled some papers from his briefcase. "I need to go over some of your financial investments. Do you feel up for it?

As Brian turned to face him, Matthew noted that his eyes were red as if he had been crying. It touched Matthew that Brian would get so emotional on his behalf. Matthew prayed that he would listen to the truth before it was too late.

Claire came in while Matthew and Brian were reviewing a large stack of papers. "I'm sorry to bother you, Brian, but I need to give you some medication. Can I interrupt for just a moment or come back later?"

"Do whatever you damn well, please," Brian barked.

"Excuse me? Have I done something to upset you?" Claire asked, truly puzzled.

"Yeah, you have. You and your Jesus freak friend who are almighty and judgmental. The world does not revolve around your so-called principles, you know. This is still my house, and I don't appreciate your greater than thou attitude towards me or people I consider my family."

"I'm sorry you feel that way, and I apologize if we came off as judgmental. None of us are perfect, and we certainly don't want to project that. We do, however, have a belief system that we are passionate about. We don't push our beliefs on others unless invited, but you need to understand that Whisper grew up in a church and chose for herself to follow that same belief system. How Marcy reacted is the same way any parent would react—she was disappointed. But that doesn't change her love for her daughter or for Matthew. Surely you can see that."

"Whatever, I don't think I will ever understand you people. Just do me a favor, do what you need to do and then leave us alone for a while."

Claire gave Brian his medication and left. She really wanted to see if Matthew had heard from Jack but decided to ask after his meeting with Brian. Maybe she would just have to break down and call Jack personally. She felt as if this whole saga was a black cloud hanging over all their heads and making everyone tense.

She walked down to the beach and sat staring at the ocean. "How did you do it, Lord? To walk among us and stay perfect in all you did? To be among sin and temptation and the hurt you endured for a world that hated you. Yet you still offered love to all those who asked. You still died to save us even when the world spit on you. I'm not sure I will ever fully comprehend the magnitude of your love, but I will forever be thankful. I pray you continue to guide me, speak words through me to bring him to you. I am sure that is my purpose here, help me, Lord. Take this cloud of doubt, anger, and sadness away so that he can open his eyes and heart to hear your truth." She stood, brushed off the sand, and decided to go back and FaceTime her own grandkids. That always brightened her mood; and right now, that is what she needed most. She saw Marcy and Whisper walking through the garden hand in hand, smiling, laughing and gave a prayer of thanks that they were working things out.

Ernesto had done a good job of spreading the happy news. Not everyone had met Matthew, and no one had met Whisper before, but they had all felt as if they knew them both from stories they had heard. One by one, they had all made their way to the main house to offer their congratulations to the happy couple throughout the next morning. The day was beautiful—dry, sunny, and a cool breeze came in off the ocean. They all decided to have lunch outside with an impromptu barbecue. Claire made sure to set up picnic tables within view from Brian's window. If he wanted to be upset and be miserable, that was up to him. She wanted to show him that even though families argue and fight, they were still family and supported each other through thick and thin. He had been less talkative the night before, but at least he had let her care for him without too much attitude.

Claire felt a peace flow through her as she watched the children play and heard the laughter and giggles. She asked Gerard if he would go inside with her and see if Brian wanted to come out to join the festivities. Surprisingly his sour mood had lifted, and he was eager to join. Once they hit the porch, the other men came over to help lift the wheelchair down the stairs and push him through the grass to a seat at the head of the table. No one mentioned the tenseness from earlier, and Claire noticed a tenderness in the way he looked at everyone. She gently placed her hand on his arm and was pleasantly surprised when he grabbed it and squeezed. He looked at her with a longing like she had never seen.

"I'm sorry if I was rude to you. You have to understand that this right here is all I ever wanted. These are my people and the closest thing to family I have ever had. I become very defensive if I think any of them are hurt in any way."

"I completely understand, Brian. And I hope you know that everyone here feels the same about you." Claire let him hold her hand. She saw him decline slowly day by day and was once again taken aback when she looked closely and saw a completely different man from just a few short months before. He was wasting away slowly, and once again, she wasn't sure how long he would be with them.

"Maybe you Jesus freaks do have it right. In my family, anyone who disagreed with us or argued was just dismissed and never thought of again. The whole idea of forgiving someone who hurt you was never an option. Maybe I need to reconsider some things." He gave Claire a sad smile. "No matter what else, I do believe you and Marcy were sent here for a reason. Whether it be from fate, the universe, or your God, I am grateful. I have learned more about real love from you two than I ever thought possible, so thank you."

Both Claire and Brian had tears in their eyes. "We are just as grateful for you, Brian. We are not perfect, but we are filled with a perfect love. And I pray every day that you will find that for yourself." She wiped her eyes, cleared her throat, and started helping put food on the table. This time, when they all joined hands for the meal prayer, Brian not only grabbed her hand and bowed his head but actually said "Amen" and squeezed her hand after the prayer.

With the exception of Whisper and Matthew spending more time on their phones than actually interacting with the others, the afternoon was better than any of them could have hoped for. Claire found a shady spot for Brian where he slept off and on but kept a smile on his face the entire day. John and Isabelle's twins, Jasmine and John Junior, were keeping everyone entertained with music and silly games. It was quite funny to watch Gerard playing hopscotch and potato sack races. Jake was happy playing fetch with Tank and kept close to his mom, obviously shy around Brian.

Claire watched Tank closely and had noted that he stuck pretty close to Brian in the last week. She couldn't help herself from a few tears when Brian, leaning back in his wheelchair with eyes closed, sensed Tank beside him and reached down to pet his head softly. It would always amaze her at how animals knew instinctively when people were dying or needed them. The entire day was happy, emotional, and heartbreaking all at once. She took a deep breath and began cleaning up. She had to separate herself and be alone for a bit to compose herself. It was always so difficult when she became so attached to her patients, and this case was even more so since she was caring for him and living on the compound.

She was in the kitchen washing dishes when she heard the crowd celebrating outside. She walked on the porch in time to see Matthew on the phone with one fist pumping in the air and everyone laughing and smiling.

She stepped up by Marcy and asked, "Why is everyone celebrating?"

"Matthew just got a call from Jack. I am not sure what they are talking about, but Matthew looked over to Brian and just said 'He did it. He got proof you didn't kill anyone.' The look of relief on Brian's face was priceless."

Claire made her way around the crowd surrounding Matthew and found Brian. He didn't look relieved at the moment, he looked unresponsive. Claire grabbed Gerard and had him help her take Brian into the house. His head bobbed up and down, and he didn't wake up even with the bumpy grass and stairs. He had lost so much weight that Claire and Gerard easily lifted him from the wheelchair and into the bed. Gerard shot Claire a worried look. "Is he gone?"

"No, he still has a pulse, but this is not good. He isn't responding at all," Claire said as she got busy getting his vital signs and performing an assessment.

"Should I go tell the others?" Gerard was pale and sweating heavily.

"No, let's not ruin the happy mood just yet. Go on back out to the party and when you can get Matthew alone, tell him to come in, please. Are you okay, Gerard?" Claire was worried he might pass out.

"I am just worried, ma'am. I thought I was ready for this, but maybe I am not."

"Let me take care of him. I don't know if this is actually his time yet. He has surprised us before when I didn't think he would pull through." She tried to sound reassuring.

Claire got busy getting Brian comfortable. He didn't show any signs of pain, but his breathing was slightly labored, and he had fluid in his lungs when she listened. His temperature was high, but his arms and legs were cool to the touch. His blood pressure was low, but his pulse was very rapid. She knew from experience that the signs he was showing were not promising. At some point, Tank had lumbered

141

in and would not leave his bedside. Claire had to practically jump over him, and he wouldn't budge even when she scolded him.

She gave him some medication to slow his heart rate and improve his breathing and then grabbed some cool washcloths to place behind his neck. She reached down to brush his hair and then grabbed his hand.

"Heavenly Father, I am asking you to give him enough time to accept you. I feel he is close, and just like the thief who was hung beside you, I would love to see Brian join you in paradise. I know as long as he is breathing, he has that opportunity. Thank you, Lord, for the opportunity to care of another one of your children."

She prayed out loud and knew Brian had heard her pray. She knew better than any of them that the dying can hear everything right up to the last minute.

Claire heard Marcy yelling for her down the hall, "Hey, missy, you are missing out on the celebrating out there? Why in tarnation would you bring our boy in here instead of out there joining in? Why, good Lord knows…" She stopped short when she saw Brian. "Oh my heavens above… don't you tell me he is dead! Not now, not now!" She cried.

Claire gently guided Marcy back out into the hall. "Marcy, it's okay. He isn't gone just yet. I hate to ruin the celebration, but I need to go out and tell the others that if they want to say their goodbyes, they need to do so now. Will you sit with him while I do that? Maybe you could say yours while you are here."

Marcy looked at Claire and then started sobbing. "No, I can't. I can't. If I say goodbye, then he will die!"

Claire enveloped Marcy in a fierce hug, "Oh, my beautiful friend. He is going to die whether we say goodbye or not. We love him, all of us do. Let him know how he has touched you. I will give you some time. He may not be responding, but he can hear you."

"How can this be? He was just outside with us! He was laughing and smiling. He was smiling less than a half hour ago! How can this happen so fast? I don't understand this at all." She sobbed.

Claire kept holding her for another few minutes then gently guided her to a chair at Brian's bedside. She placed Marcy's hand in Brian's and kissed her forehead then left the room.

"This is the part of the job I dread the most, Lord, help me say the right words." She prayed to herself as she walked out to tell the others.

She approached Ernesto first in hopes that he could support Marcy as well. Gerard had already told Matthew, and when she looked over at him, he was on the phone but nodded at her; and she could tell he was dealing with business, so she walked over to Whisper.

"I take it Matthew knows the latest development?" Claire asked.

"Yes, he is on the phone right now with the studios," Whisper replied softly. "They have been calling him almost daily for the last month, but Matt didn't want to give any information about Brian's condition. Brian asked that nothing be said until he was gone. I wish I could have met Brian in person sooner. He is so different from the man I have dealt with on the phone and from what I imagined him to be."

"Actually he is a different man from when we first arrived, Whisper. He had such a protective wall around his heart and soul. I think the man we have come to know is who he always was but wouldn't let anyone else see."

"I think he let Matt see his true self. Matt has always been very adamant that Brian was different than the persona others saw. I thought he was crazy for putting up with Brian's demands and abrasive attitude for so long. I guess I should've trusted Matt's instincts."

The group slowly made their way in and congregated in the sunroom after they had said their goodbyes. Claire was careful to give them space individually but made sure she could check in with him and asked that they keep their visits short for the time being.

Matt was the last one to visit Brian, and Claire really wanted to talk to him about his conversation with Jack but wasn't sure if this was the right time. She knew that Matthew would take Brian's death hard and wanted to give him space to deal with his own grief. At the same time, Claire was curious as to why she hadn't heard from Jack herself. She knew she could call Jack and ask him directly; and several times, she picked up her phone to do so but always stopped short and chickened out at the last minute.

As she looked around the room, she felt very alone for the first time in a long time. Marcy was leaning on Ernesto. Whisper was sitting with Matthew, gently rubbing his back. Gerard and Sable were holding hands, and John and Isabelle had their children on their laps. Tank must have sensed her discomfort and lopped over, tongue hanging out with slobber dribbling, and laid his head on her lap. She laughed and hugged him tightly, breaking the solemn silence. He reached up and licked her face causing the kids to giggle as Claire let out a loud, "Ewww! I love you, buddy, but that's gross!"

Gerard stood, cleared his throat, and surprised them all with a commanding voice, "Okay, enough of this. Mr. Montgomery would be mortified to see us all out here bemoaning on his behalf. Let's pull ourselves together and get back to what we all do best. I am sure Ms. Claire will let us know if she needs us, but we have arrangement and preparations to do. It is getting late, and I am sure everyone is tired and emotionally drained from our day. Let's get a good night's rest, and then tomorrow we will get to work. I am sure we will have an influx of visitors soon, and we need to ensure that the grounds and estate is presentable and ready. Make a list of items you need and give it to Sable. We will make a trip into town and gather supplies. Matthew, can you make a list of people who might need other accommodations and an estimated account of who will be staying on the estate?"

Matthew and Gerard moved to the office while others began working on cleanup from the day's activities. Whisper, not knowing what to do, gave Claire a quizzical look.

"You have had quite an active few days, Whisper. How about a swim or a long hot bubble bath?"

"Sounds wonderful, Aunt Claire, you don't mind? I am happy to pitch in if I can help."

"You can help by taking care of that special bundle. Between the stress of telling Marcy, all the travel, and now all this, you need some rest. Go, please, we can handle all this." Claire gave her a reassuring hug and headed for the library.

Brian's breathing was less labored, but his blood pressure was still very low with a very fast heart rate, and he was not responding at all. Claire sat beside him, grabbed his hand, and began reading the Bible to him.

She told him about how Moses had murdered someone and was a poor speaker but still led Israel out of Egypt and freed thousands from slavery. David had a man killed to commit adultery, yet became king and one of God's chosen. She read stories of how God used Paul who condemned Christians but became an apostle and one of the greatest missionaries and preachers of the New Testament. She read to him for hours and would encourage him that it was never too late. She worried that she was crossing an ethical nursing boundary; but at the same time, she no longer worked for a company, and Brian knew her beliefs and even hinted that he wanted to know more.

She heard a soft knock on the door as Gerard and Matthew came in, looking disheveled and tired. Claire looked at the clock and saw that it was well past midnight.

"I think both of you need to get some rest. You look terrible." Claire smiled weakly.

"I think you are right, Ms. Claire. But we just wanted to check in. Has there been any change?" Gerard asked.

"Not much, really. He is still very close, and I don't expect him to make it through the night. However, it would be great if you two got some sleep. I may need relief at some point."

"Claire." Matthew sighed. "I know you well enough by now that you could really use a swim or a walk. Since it is too late for a walk, how about if you go for a quick swim, and then I promise I will go up and get some rest. Just because you are the nurse doesn't mean you are the only one with common sense. Plus I would like a few minutes alone with him."

"Thank you, Matthew. You know me too well for someone who doesn't know me very well." She laughed.

"You'd be surprised at the stories Whisper has told me." He winked.

Gerard had been standing close to Brian, and he squeezed his hand and turned to walk out the door. His head was low, and he was obviously crying but not wanting the other two seeing him. Matthew patted him on the back as he slipped out of the room.

"I don't think he realized just how hard this would be." Matthew looked at the closed door. "To be honest, neither did I. Go take a swim or a short nap, Claire. I will be okay, really," he said when she gave him a look as if to say she didn't believe him.

"Okay, but I will leave my cell phone close. Call me if you need me." Claire took advantage of the quiet, changed quickly, and headed for the pool. She closed her eyes, floated on her back for a while then turned to lean on the pool's edge and began sobbing. No matter how long she had done this job, it didn't get easier to say goodbye. She cared deeply for every patient, but Brian was special. She began to swim laps hard and fast.

When she was thoroughly exhausted, she stopped and sat on the ladder. Only then did she look up to see someone sitting and watching her.

"Jack!" She jumped up, climbed the ladder quickly, and ran into his arms.

"I am so glad to see you, but so angry at the same time! Why didn't you call me? I didn't know anything about what happened or what you found out. I still don't. You promised you would stay in touch, and then nothing. Why didn't you call me?" She sobbed and yelled at the same time. "Sorry, I am getting you all wet."

"It's okay, lovely Claire. I don't mind getting wet, it just feels good to hold you." He whispered softly into her wet head.

She pulled back away and began swatting at his chest. "You truly are an exasperating man, you know!"

He laughed softly. "I have a lot to tell you, but I wanted to give you some space. I didn't want to be too pushy. Plus I got rather busy."

"I need to relieve Matthew. Let me change my clothes, and I will meet you down in the library, okay?"

He kissed the top of her head. "Sounds good, see you there."

Ten minutes later, dressed in pajamas and a robe, Claire joined Matthew and Jack. She checked on Brian first. His breathing had really slowed, and he was having apnea periods.

"He freaks me out when he stops breathing like that. I keep thinking he is gone, and then he starts breathing again. Is that normal?" Matthew asked.

"Yes, it is. It is called apnea, and right now, his episodes are lasting about fifteen seconds. Pretty soon, they will get longer. I am so sorry, Matthew, but he is very close."

"Okay, well, I am going to check on Whisper and try to get some sleep. Call me if he umm, you know."

"I will, I promise." Claire hugged him tightly.

When Matthew was gone, she asked Jack to pull up a chair beside her.

"Okay, tell me everything. Don't leave out a single detail."

"What? No concern about my getting rest?" Jack teased.

"Not a bit." She smiled. "I can't tell you the last time I slept more than two hours at a time, so you get no sympathy from me, bucko."

"Aye, I see how it is, Ms. Sassy. Okay, where to start? When I arrived, I really didn't know what to expect or what I was really looking for. I started with local spots and began searching for anyone that looked like that drawing. I wrote you a lot of letters, sitting in those smoky bars Claire." He chuckled and squeezed her hand.

"Will you ever show them to me?" she asked.

"Maybe someday. But I digress. I started hanging around the docks. I didn't want to seem like I was snooping, so I told the dockmaster that I needed a small cabin cruiser to rent while I was working on a book. It worked. Within a week, I not only found your mysterious stalker from the yacht, but I also found Peter. Apparently Peter was running a similar scam on quite a few people and had gone from yacht captain to living in a lap of luxury. He had his own yacht, and your stalker was working as his bodyguard."

"What? I don't understand. If the guy knew Peter was a scammer, why didn't he blackmail him and get in on the action?"

"Well, it seems he tried, but he was a drunk and a gambler which actually made it very easy to get information out of him. When Peter was stateside, he worked for many of the rich and famous like Brian. He played the game very well, and then he met player number 2, Rich Hughes."

"Who's that?" Claire asked. "The name sounds vaguely familiar."

"Have you lived in a cave for the last decade, my love? He is a celebrity gossip writer."

"Oh yes, that is who Brian went out on the yacht with that night, right?" Claire's internal light bulb switched on.

"Exactly. So the two of them met, and Rich noticed that Peter is connected with all these people he wants to interview. Peter started setting up these interviews, and they built a relationship. So one night when they were out, drinking and crying in their beers how they are tired of being surrounded by all this wealth, and they were each struggling to make ends meet. So they came up with the scheme to stage Rich's murder and blackmail the hit list."

"So Rich Hughes is alive?" Jack leaned back and rubbed his eyes.

"Very much so, although he does have a slightly different look. I am guessing he should have chosen a plastic surgeon closer to the states because the one he chose did a bags job. His nose is pretty gammy."

"Sorry?" Claire looked puzzled.

"Chop job, you know, messed up plastics."

"Oh, umm, okay."

"I really must teach you proper slang." Jack laughed.

Brian stirred, and Claire got up to check on him.

"Should I leave or be quieter?" Jack asked.

"No, not at all. In fact, you should speak up. Hearing is the last sense to go, and I have a strong feeling that he has only held on this long to hear this story. He collapsed almost immediately after you called Matthew to give him the news."

"Really? Wow. Okay. So where was I?"

"Rich's botched plastic surgery," Claire answered as she was positioning Brian and fluffing pillows.

"Oh, right. So it was a little difficult for Richie to stage his own murder, video, and take pictures. Peter can't do it because he has to drive the boat, drug the stook, and set up the whole thing. So they hired Richie's photographer and promised to cut him in on the deal. The beauty is that no one knew who he is, and he came in after the dupe is passed out and took the blackmail pictures."

"But doesn't anyone get suspicious if they are doing this over and over?"

"That's the beauty of it. They spend two weeks doing the same act to at least twenty people that I could track down. Then Rich heads off to the islands to hang out and wait for the checks to start pouring in. He set up foreign accounts to filter the money, and the three of them end up banking over fifty grand a month."

"So why didn't Peter join him earlier?"

"Because he is playing the odds that no one is going to the coppers or talking to each other. So he has to keep an eye on the operation and keep tabs on his teabags. But then Bruno, the photographer, starts getting greedy and spending too much on gambling and floozies, so he tries to blackmail Peter and Richie. That's when the threads start unraveling. And to top it off, Peter gets wind that two old biddies are snooping around the yacht and stirring up doubts in Brian. Plus the eejit Bruno is following Peter around, causing a ruckus."

Claire laughed. "Remind me to have a dictionary handy when you tell a story. So Bruno, is that his real name?"

Jack smiled. "Nah, but Roger doesn't make a great story now, does it?"

Claire just shook her head. "No, I suppose not. So Bruno actually tried to blackmail the blackmailers?"

"Righto, but he is a little dense and just ended up screwing the whole operation up. That mixed with your little encounter, Peter decides to go incognito and start to enjoy the fruits of his labor like Richie is doing. They actually did a fairly good job of lying low but were enjoying their new found wealth a little too much and don't handle their liquor well. It wasn't too hard to piece things together especially after offering a big paycheck to Bruno who spilled the beans pretty quickly when he thought he could turn the tables on them."

"Wow, just wow. I am so thankful you were able to figure it all out before it was too late. I would hate for Brian to have his image damaged like this."

"Well, that's the gist of it. But as much as I would love to just sit here and yarn a little more to the tale, I really am knackered and need some shut eye." Jack yawned and stretched.

"Thank you, and thank you for telling me the story here so he can hear. Go get some rest but leave me some of your coffee so I can make you some when you get up." She jabbed him in the shoulder.

"Well, I suppose I could share. I'll leave it in the cupboard. Try and get some rest yourself, lovie."

He kissed her on the forehead and gently hugged her. After he left, she got a washrag and began stroking Brian's head. "I knew you couldn't murder anyone, you big lug. Now all you need is to make it right with God, and you will be able to spend eternity in peace and a happiness you have never known here on earth."

She said a prayer over him and squeezed his hand. His skin was cold, and she knew he wouldn't make it until morning. She gave him medication and curled up with a book in the window seat. She was beyond exhausted but suddenly felt at peace herself and closed her eyes. Her book wasn't even cracked open before she was sound asleep.

Exactly ninety-four minutes after she had closed her eyes, she suddenly was wide awake and rushed over to Brian. She knew before she checked that he was gone. The look on his face was so incredibly peaceful, it took her breath away. She could only hope and pray that he was seeing heaven in his final moments. She cried as she went through the motions of checking for a heartbeat, documenting the time, calling the doctor for permission to pronounce, and calling the coroner. Because Brian was on hospice, an autopsy wasn't necessary, and she was given approval to call the crematory. She knew she needed to wake up Gerard and Matthew but was dreading it. She wanted some time alone with him. She grabbed a notebook and began to journal as many good memories as she could. It always helped her to keep their memories going and how each patient touched her life in their own unique way.

Eventually she sent a text to everyone so as not to have to knock on doors. Plus she wasn't exactly sure where everyone was sleeping. Within five minutes, the entire group was surrounding Brian's bed, holding hands, and singing both hymns and some of Brian's favorite secular songs. It was an hour before the mortuary came, and not one person left his side. Tears and exhaustion filled everyone. No one cared that they were all in pajamas, hair messy, no makeup. This was a family; and as Claire scanned the room, she realized why Brian was so emphatic about dying here among his people. His life was alone and empty except when he was here.

Claire suddenly felt very sad knowing that her time, her job here was done. She was very anxious to get out of the Florida heat and humidity and was longing to be back in Colorado with her own family, but her heart was heavy at the thought of leaving these people she had grown to love so deeply. As if reading her mind, Marcy came up beside her and wrapped her arm around Claire's waist.

"I know this isn't a good time to talk about it, but I am not leaving yet. I know the girls have been patient, and you are anxious to get out to see them, so you go."

"Ernesto doesn't want you to leave yet, I am sure of that." Claire smiled at her friend.

"I am not sure if this will lead into anything, but I am too old not to grab every opportunity I have to find someone to spend what time God gives me with." Marcy chuckled.

"You deserve happiness, Marcy. There is no reason you shouldn't stay. I will let the girls know that you won't be joining me. To be honest, I was just thinking I am not quite ready to leave either. Although I can't wait to get back to some tolerable heat."

"Amen to that, sister, I may melt before you return. Poor Whisper, I can remember being pregnant during a Florida summer. At least she isn't showing too much."

"Let's get everyone out of this room and into the kitchen to make some coffee. We could all use some right now as I don't see any of us being able to go back to bed just yet."

"Sounds like a plan, Stan." Marcy winked.

Jack, Matthew, and Whisper got busy on their phones. Sable, Isabelle, Marcy, and Claire worked in unison to make a lovely breakfast. Claire really wasn't hungry, so once everyone grabbed food, she snuck out to go for a swim. She had hoped that she was stealthy enough for no one to notice her absence. She had changed quickly and got a good fifteen minutes in of hard laps before she looked up and saw Jack watching her.

"You do realize that you have made spying on me swimming a bad habit, don't you?" She smiled.

"I wouldn't consider it a bad habit at all. In fact, I use this image as a daily meditation now," he joked.

Claire found herself relaxed and laughing easily at his flirting. "I think I need to research you some better meditation visuals. You are always outside the pool. Don't you swim?"

"Aye, but lately, I enjoy watching you more. I am not as strong as you are, and I wouldn't want to embarrass myself. I mostly just float."

"Nothing wrong with that, I like to float before and after laps too."

He sat down on the edge and dangled his legs in the water. She swam up to the edge and placed her arms on the ledge, far enough away that she could work her legs without hitting his. Neither said anything for a few minutes and just enjoyed the quiet. Tank ambled up next to Jack and placed his head in his lap while Jack just reached down and petted him, causing Tank to roll on his side, precariously close to the edge.

"What will he do if he rolls over and into the pool?" Jack asked.

Claire laughed. "Swim to the steps as fast as his big butt will take him and go sulk for a while. He has done it before, and he doesn't like it. But he can swim pretty well for a big guy."

Jack sighed. "I will be heading out tomorrow. Not sure where the winds will carry me, but I have done the job here and am no longer needed."

Claire nodded. "Same here. I am not sure how soon I will leave, but my job is done too. I am anxious to see my kids and grandkids but a little sad to leave. This has been a wonderful experience, and these people feel like family now."

"I am sure you can stay as long as you would like, love. They feel the same about you."

"My husband loved the humidity and heat. And while I like Florida most of the time, summer is not my favorite season here. I prefer the dry air in the mountains with cool nights no matter what season."

"Sounds wonderful. I used to live next to the mountains in Italy for a while. Winters were rainy and cool but never as harsh as Colorado."

"You have obviously never lived there. It really isn't bad at all."

"Maybe I will venture there sometime especially now that I have a reason." He sounded sad.

"Maybe you will get an invite. We definitely have plenty of rooms." She smiled. She wasn't sure what to say, she wasn't ready to say goodbye to him, but she didn't want a relationship either.

"Tell me about it, your place out there."

She pulled herself up and sat on the edge next to him. He reached behind Tank and grabbed her a towel.

"It's lovely, really. It started off as a project for my husband and me. We bought an old farmhouse that I thought was charming, and it had a lot of acreage with it. We built a small kit house first so we could live on the property while remodeling the main house. We thought the kit house would make a nice guesthouse when we were done. It took a long time, a lot of sweat and hard work, but we eventually got the main house finished, thinking we would turn it into a bed and breakfast when we retired. But things changed. Dirk was offered that job, and he thought the project would take him into retirement. He loved remodeling the main house and decided to buy the house here in Florida as a vacation home that we rented out when we weren't here for income. Anyway my daughters were going through a rough time, and we ended up moving the girls on the property and letting them run it. They are very good at it too. They have successfully made it into a profitable business. We bought it when the land was fairly inexpensive, and it has almost quadrupled in value. After my husband died, Matthew took an interest and has helped the girls expand. We now have several cabins and a community garden. There are hiking areas, lakes and trails close by, and skiing is only about an hour away. So they stay busy year-round."

"Wow, sounds impressive. Maybe I will have to check it out. So you are a nurse, a fabulous cook, a successful business owner... is there anything you can't do?"

"I just supplied the business, my girls are the ones that make it run. I do admit, I enjoy reaping the benefits a few months a year. God has blessed me more than I ever deserved. What about you? Where do you call home?"

"London for the last year, before that Australia. I have a bit of wanderlust and have difficulty settling down to one spot. I too have been blessed, and my job allows me to travel so much that nowhere is really home. It's just a flat where I hang out until the next job. Although I admit that I am ready to hang it up. Truth is, I only did this job for Mattie as a favor because I thought it would be quick, relatively safe and easy. As much as I have traveled, I really haven't been able to experience any of the places I have been."

"A small part of me envies that lifestyle. I love to travel too, but I also love coming home. And I try not to go this long without seeing the grandkids. They grow up so fast. I feel like I worked so much when my girls were young and missed a lot, I didn't want to make that mistake with the grands. But I probably haven't done a great job at that either. The oldest two are already grown and off doing their own things."

"Yoo-hoo... am I interrupting anything?" Marcy yelled from the door.

"Not at all, come join us," Claire yelled back.

"Claire, I know you are exhausted but can you come help? We could use some extra hands. Jack, Matthew was looking for you too."

Jack yelled back, "Be right there." He looked over at Claire. "I would love to spend some more one-on-one time with you before I go. How about dinner in town tonight, just the two of us?"

"Maybe, depends on whether I get some sleep in today. I am running on fumes right now, but the swim helped, so it's a definite possibility. Do you have to leave tomorrow? Is there any reason you can't extend it for another day?"

Jack smiled, and his entire face lit up. "I am sure I can manage that." He reached over to kiss her, and she turned her cheek.

"That would be lovely. We better get in before they send a search party."

The kitchen was a flurry of action when they walked in. "What's going on? How can I help?"

Sable looked at Claire with a desperate expression and tear-filled eyes. "Oh, Ms. Claire. I don't think any of us realized the amount of people that would be flying in for Mr. Montgomery's service. Gerard has specifically told them that Mr. Montgomery did not want a large service, but no one is listening. I am not sure where we will put all these people."

Claire reached over and grabbed Sable's hand. "Breathe, my friend. First of all, if people choose to come, it is not your responsibility to feed and house them. Brian ran in some elite circles, and I am sure they can make other accommodations. Having a service here is one thing but don't expect to supply them all with rooms. The staff here was Brian's family, and those should be the only ones staying on the grounds. Secondly there are catering services I am sure we can employ for the food. Where is Gerard? I will go talk to him."

"He is in his office with Mr. Matthew. Thank you, Ms. Claire, I just don't want to disappoint Mr. Montgomery. Even though he is no longer with us, this is still his home. Oh, what are we going to do without him?" Sable cried.

"You need time to grieve, Sable. Go on, go for a walk, go into your room to cry for a while, just go do something for yourself. I promise, the rest will work itself out." Claire hugged her tightly.

Claire knocked on Gerard's office door and found him pacing back and forth on the phone. Matthew shaking his head back and forth, talking to someone on his cell phone. Both were so engrossed in their conversations that they did not even notice Claire enter. Claire cleared her throat loudly, and they both looked at her incredulously with eyebrows raised. She mouthed, "Get off the phone." And both relented and ended their conversations.

Matthew looked at her. "What is it, Claire? We are both a little busy here."

"That's exactly what I want to talk to you about. You both know that Brian did not want a circus. He didn't even want people to know he was sick. What are you two planning that you have Sable all worked up about trying to house and feed everyone?"

Gerard bowed his head. "I am sorry, Ms. Claire, but this has turned into exactly that. His publicist, manager, and studio director are all demanding a large service. Within one hour, we have about a thousand people coming, and I don't know how to tell them no."

"Well, that's simple," Claire retorted. "Tell them if they want to plan a large service, that's fine but they can do it in Hollywood where there isn't a strain on his family. Matthew, I can't believe you of all people are letting those celebrities push you around like that."

"That's brilliant, Claire, thank you. I don't think either one of us are thinking at all right now. We are numb. I mean, we expected this, but is anyone really prepared when the time comes?"

"No, not really." Claire reached over to rub Matthew's shoulders. "Gerard, call the publicist and manager back. Tell them that there will be no service at this residence. If they want a big service, then let someone else plan it. That's why they were paid so much. It's the least they can do for all the money Brian made them. Be forceful but realize they are being blindsided by all this."

Gerard smiled, nodded his head, and got back on the phone.

"Should we really ship him out to California for a service he never wanted?" Matthew asked.

"Of course not," Claire answered. "They can rent a casket and just keep it empty. I am sure they have plenty of photos they can blow up and place around it. Brian was adamant that he wanted to be cremated and that he didn't want a media frenzy here. That's what we need to keep in mind."

Gerard got off the phone, his face was flushed. "Well, they aren't happy about it but agreed. Ms. Claire, I heard you were planning on leaving tomorrow. Would you be willing to stay for just a few more days to help us? None of us has been through something like this. We could use your experience and input."

"Of course, Gerard. I haven't even checked flight schedules yet. I can call the kids and let them know I will head out next week."

Both Gerard and Matthew came around to hug her tightly. "I don't know what he would have done without you here. Thank you, Claire, for all you have done. You have no idea how much it means to all of us. You gave him dignity and peace these last few months. I know you weren't thrilled to take this job, but I thank God every day that you and Marcy were here."

"Me, too, Matt. Me too. Now if you gentlemen don't mind, I think I would like to take a nap. We have a lot of details to clear up, and I really need some rest."

Claire went up and laid in bed without even showering or changing out of her swimsuit. She curled up and was out like a light within seconds after her head hit the pillow.

Matthew took Claire's advice to heart. He ordered everyone to take a few hours to themselves and meet back at the main house for dinner. He called a local restaurant and ordered enough food for everyone. Then he went to find his wife. Funny that was the first time he really called her his wife in his head. It felt good, it felt right. There was so much he wanted to talk to her about. He found her in the sunroom lightly sleeping on the swing. He gently lifted her head and sat placing her head on his lap. She reached over and squeezed his leg. "Do I need to get up?" She yawned.

"Don't even think about it unless you would like to go lie down somewhere more comfortable." He said stroking her hair.

"No, I am okay. Everyone has treated me with kid gloves, and I am probably the only one who has gotten plenty of sleep in the last two days. What can I do for you? Let me help you, please."

"I have everything I need right here. I am exhausted, but there is no way I can sleep. Wanna go for a walk? I have some ideas I would like to run by you."

"I would love that." They walked hand in hand in silence, down the well-worn path to the beach. As they got to the clearing, they noticed that they were not the only ones with the same idea. Ernesto and Marcy were sitting on a large rock, staring at the ocean and oblivious to their surroundings. Whisper grabbed Matthew's arm, placed her finger over her lips to indicate not to say anything and pointed back to the path. They walked back and as soon as she was sure she was out of earshot, she giggled.

"Sorry, but I feel a little silly barging in on my mother's private moment. I just couldn't break their moment. It feels so nice to see her so happy and engulfed in her own romance rather than being that way in mine."

He kissed the top of her head. "I couldn't agree more, my dear." They found a quiet spot in the courtyard and sat on the fountain ledge.

"Okay, spill it. What would you like to talk about? I know this trip is probably the hardest one you have made in your career. You have worked for Mr.... I mean Brian, for so long. How are you holding up?"

"I can't deny I am shaken. I told Claire I was prepared but really, I am not sure I was. I am just pretty numb right now."

"I get that. Our careers have literally revolved around him for so long. What are we going to do?"

"That's what I wanted to talk to you about. Once you start showing more, we won't be able to hide our baby or our relationship at the office. To be honest, I don't want to either. You have been my other half in the office for so long, I don't think I want to replace you either. What do you say we start our own practice?"

"Matt, are you kidding? I would love that! How would that work though? I am not a lawyer. I am just a glorified secretary. I can't help you much."

"I think you take yourself too lightly. You are smarter and know more about the law than most lawyers I know. I know you secretly always wanted to go to law school. Do you still want to?"

"I am not sure anymore, to be honest. I don't know if I want to take all that time and energy away from our baby. Maybe someday, but I don't think I could think about it just now. Would that disappoint you?"

"Not at all. In fact, it isn't really practical at this point in our lives, but then nothing we have done so far is really practical." They both chuckled.

"I think I make a pretty good administrative assistant though, and I can work really hard for you until our little nugget is born. After that, we can decide what we want to do to expand. I know of at least five clients that love you and would follow you into private practice."

"Yes, and I think I want to be a little more specific about clientele as well. I don't want another Brian that is going to take so much time away from you and the baby. I want to find a place where we can raise a family and maybe just open a small practice to start."

"I love that idea. And I love you, Matthew Harper. Thank you for thinking of us. When should I call and resign?"

"You can call today if you want. I won't resign until I am sure all of Brian's affairs are in order. That may take several months. We have enough in savings to get us by with both of us not working for a couple of years, although I don't really want to test that. Let's take it one day at a time with a goal in mind. I just wanted to discuss the possibilities with you."

"I am excited. You have made me the luckiest bride. I am so blessed to have you."

"I love you, too, Whisper, and feel equally blessed. I never thought I could be this happy."

"Let's go back, and I will fix you some chamomile tea so you can get some rest."

"Aren't I supposed to be the one worrying about you and the baby?"

"You do that too much. I am fine. Let me take care of you just this once."

chapter
11

Marcy couldn't take the silence much longer. She and Ernesto had been sitting there for over an hour. She could only stare at water for so long before getting antsy. "Come on, dear. I need to move."

"Mi amor, there are things we need to discuss," Ernesto said.

"I know that, silly. But there is no reason we can't walk while we talk."

"Si, but I want to look in your eyes to see if your answers are true."

"I gave you my word from the very beginning, Ernie, that I would not lie to you. I am too old to play games. But if it makes you feel any better, I have no intention of leaving with Claire. I already told her I need to see where our relationship will go. I am committed to you to find out, so if that is what you are worried about then don't get all morose on me."

"I do not know this word *moonrose*. But yes, that is what I want to talk about. I want to get married. I cannot think of another day without you. I have plenty of money and have talked to Gerard. We can stay here for as long as we need to make plans for our future together."

"Oh, good Lord in heavens, yes. Of course, I will marry you. Look out world, another Lucy and Ricky are headed your way!" She laughed and hugged him tightly.

"I do not understand you most of the time, but I hope to spend the rest of my life finding out," he said as he kissed her deeply.

Marcy was on top of the world. She felt like God had given her the most beautiful gift on such a sad day. She sent up a thank you prayer for Brian, for Claire, and the incredible mercy and grace that gave her such a gift as this.

They all gathered in the dining room at seven sharp. Most of the group had taken a nap or some personal time, and everyone looked a little more refreshed and relaxed. Sable had taken special care to set the room very formal, like one of the dinner parties Mr. Montgomery held for special occasions. They all laughed and told stories of their time spent together and with Brian. When they were finished eating, Matthew cleared his throat loudly, stood up, and clinked his glass.

"May I have everyone's attention for a moment? I would like to take this opportunity to thank you all for the love and kindness you have extended to not only my friend Brian but to my wife and me as well. I understand now why Brian chose this place to spend his last months. It has nothing to do with the beautiful house, grounds, or landscape and everything to do with who you are and who you were to him. I would very much like to read a letter he composed to you all. But before that, I want to assure you that you all have a home here. He wanted to ensure that you would all be well taken care of. Over the next few months, I will be here frequently to deal with the legalities but thought it was important to put your minds at ease. Your homes on the grounds were put into your individual names months ago." There was a visible lift of tension in the room and a few tears of relief.

Matthew pulled out a piece of paper from his jacket and began to read:

To all my friends,

I just want Matthew to let you know, you are all fired. Just kidding, I had to throw some humor from beyond. I am dead by now and can't do anything about it, but I want you all to know that I would like for you all to stay together on the grounds and continue keeping it up, maybe make it into a bed and breakfast or some useless thing for tourists. This is your home now, and I want to thank you for making this not just as one of my houses that I have collected over the years but my home as well. I think of you all as the only family that ever mattered to me. Matthew assures me that the will is set in stone, and no one can overturn it, so I hope this is enough to show my appreciation. Ernesto, I entrust you to keep the grounds as meticulous as you have for me and try not to murder children who stomp where they shouldn't and keep your nephew in school. He will go far someday. He has your brains and hard work ethic.

John and Isabelle, you both have such great talent, and I know that you stayed on here for my sake. Thank you, not just for maintaining my homes throughout the years, but your willingness to help wherever I need you.

Gerard and Sable, there are no words for my deep gratitude for all you have done for me throughout the years. I realize that I have not been the greatest boss over the years. I sincerely tried to be better since moving back here permanently and hope that you don't speak too horribly of me after I am gone.

Marcy, just keep being you. Whisper told me what Claire was paying you for helping, and I am making sure that amount is doubled. Your laughter and terrible smoothies brightened some very dark days for me. I have left for you a few signed photographs that you can show to your knitting or yoga or whatever group.

Claire, I have nothing to give you except to say I listened to your reading me the Bible, your prayers, and watched as you allowed God to shine through and show me who he really was. Rest assured, dear friend, that it was all for naught. I heard and accepted. By doing so, you actually gave me the greatest gift that I can never repay.

Jack, as I am writing this letter, I have no idea if you have resolved my situation, but I do want to thank you. The only thing that ever really mattered to me was my name, and I would prefer to have it kept not as a criminal. Thank you for working on this for me. I realize you don't know me or owe me anything, but if the case is not resolved by my death, I ask that you continue to work on it.

Whisper, take care of my boy. I know you will but just keep in mind, I don't know if I believe in ghosts or angels but know that I will be watching. As you know, he is very special to me, and I wouldn't want to have to come back to protect him. If you are anything like your mother, you will fight tooth and nail for him. Congratulations on your baby, you will both make fine parents.

Matthew will fill you in with details, but I want to make a few things clear. The stipulations to giving you your homes is non-negotiable. You must either sell to each other or Matthew should you decide to leave and fair market price will be paid. Absolutely, and I do mean absolutely, will there be no funeral held here for me on these grounds. I would like some of my ashes scattered in the courtyard and the remaining, I guess I really don't care.

To all of you, I may never have told you while I was alive because, well let's face it, I was kind of a jerk, but I sincerely love you all with every fiber of my being. You are my family, my people, and God willing, we will see each other again someday.

Brian

Matthew sat and scanned the room. He knew he couldn't read through without crying if he looked at them. He took a deep breath, raised his glass, and offered a toast.

"I will meet with you all individually to go over the will. While you are all listed in there, it is not divided equally and has more to do with how long you have worked for him and in what capacity. Claire, he wanted a large sum of money transferred to a charity of your choice. So if you could think about it and get back to me, that would be great. As far as a memorial, this is it. He was adamant about no funeral, so this is it for us. At Claire's suggestion, his publicist and manager will be planning a service in California for any of you that would like to attend. The mortuary said his ashes should be ready to pick up next week. Gerard will decide what to do with them at that time. Whisper and I will be leaving in the morning, but we will only be a phone call away if you ever need anything. As Brian said, we are a family. It is my deepest hope and prayer that we will stay so for the rest of our lives."

"Amen to that, brother," Gerard said as he raised his glass. "Might I add that the privacy contracts we all signed when we were employed does not end, and there will be no stories sold to trash magazines. I think we owe it to Mr. Montgomery to continue keeping his life private."

There was a unison of "Agreed" as they all raised their glasses.

Claire stood and asked Marcy to take a walk with her. As they reached their well-worn path, Claire put her arm around her friend. "I think everything is settled here for now. I know you are staying, so just keep in touch and let me know when I need to come back and be your maid of honor. I put some money in your account."

"Oh posh, you don't need to do that since Brian paid me. Besides, you gave me something money could never buy and that is meeting Ernie. Keep your money, you earned it," Marcy said and bumped her hip into Claire's.

"So did you, my friend, and it's already done. I truly am so happy for you. Have you thought about what you are going to do with your condo?"

"Oh heavens, no. I guess I should talk to my son-in-law. I may hang on to it for a while and do like you do, you know, rent it out on some app. Whisper can manage that for me."

"That sounds like a fine plan. I hope Ernesto knows that we still have to take our girl trips together a couple of times a year. Just because you are attached doesn't get you out of that." Claire laughed.

"Not on your life, I won't marry him if he tries to control that. We still have a lot of getting to know each other to do, honestly. Gerry and Sable are going to let me stay in the guesthouse for as long as I need, so I won't feel rushed. But I feel deep down that he is the man for me."

"I know, I do, too, or I wouldn't leave you here alone. I will miss you coming back to Colorado with me this year though."

"Are ya gonna ask Jackie boy to go?"

"No, I mean I hinted that he could come visit sometime, but I need some time with the girls and grands alone. I am not ready for a relationship yet. At least I don't think I am, and I really don't know him well enough to commit to anything. He is a nice man, and I would like to grow our friendship. But I think that is about all I can handle right now."

"When are ya gonna break his heart?"

"As soon as we get back to the house. I just wanted you in on the game plan and some private time with you first. I normally am not around for this part of the job and just needed a good stiff dose of my Marcy to pull me through. It has been a wonderful, exhausting, happy, sad, and scary roller coaster we have been on. Thank you for insisting you join me. I am not sure I would have made it through without you."

"Same here, lovey, same here."

When they arrived back at the house, everyone was on the porch, eating ice cream, laughing, and telling stories about Brian.

Marcy went up to join them and began telling the story of when they first arrived, and Brian was in the courtyard doing yoga in the buff.

Claire stood back, smiled, and caught Jack's eyes. She crooked her head and held out her hand.

He jumped up and eagerly grabbed it as they began to walk.

"Gerard doesn't really need me here if there is no big funeral to plan, so I think I will go book a flight out for tomorrow," she said as she leaned in and rested her head on his shoulder as they walked.

"So soon? I thought you were staying another week," he answered sadly.

"I know, but there really isn't much for me to do here. And I have a boatload of things to do there. It doesn't really make much sense, plus I will need to make plans to come back for Marcy and Ernesto's wedding soon, so I won't be spending as much time as I normally do in Colorado."

"So I guess this means you are just going to leave me hanging, huh? He started to pull away a little, but she held his arm tightly.

"Look, I need to tell you some things, but I can't really look at you so just let me get through this, okay?"

He squeezed her hand and nodded agreement.

"I like you a lot, and I sincerely hope we can be friends. I just don't think I am ready to get serious with anyone right now. I love my life and am very independent. If you would like, we can email, FaceTime and talk every day but give me a few weeks alone with my kids. If you would like to come visit Colorado after that, then we can talk about it. I just need time, Jack. I don't know if I can give anything back to you right now. I truly am sorry. I don't want to be hurtful, but if we are to have any kind of relationship, honesty has to be a priority."

"Aye, you're killin' me, darlin'. But I do understand, sort of. It will be good for me to sort some things out as well."

"Thank you, Jack. I don't want either of us to hurt more in the long run."

They stopped, he took her into his arms and gave her a kiss that almost made her change her mind.

"Something to remember me by," he said and gave her another small kiss.

"I will definitely remember that for a very long time," she said as they strolled back to the party.

Get ready for more of Claire and Marcy as Claire heads back to Colorado to prepare for Marcy's wedding shower and Whisper prepares for parenthood. Meet Claire's family and Marcy's daughter Sunshine as they all converge and reunite with some old friends from Missouri.

But Whisper is having difficulties with the pregnancy. She and Matthew have to make some tough decisions when they receive heart breaking news that the baby is in danger.

Marcy may have to postpone the wedding if Ernesto can't get back in time from Cuba helping his family rebuild after a hurricane.

Claire needs to decide if she is ready to take a chance on love with Jack but has concerns about his spiritual maturity and whether their relationship is really what God wants for her.

A fire breaks out at Claire's bed and breakfast with her grand-daughter missing. Is it an accident or was it set intentionally?

Find out in the next addition to the legacy series- "Hello and Goodbye in the Rockies"

ABOUT THE AUTHOR

T.C. Ryan is a hospice nurse who lives in Colorado with her husband, three adult children, grandchildren, and bulldog named Tank. She felt a calling from God to become a hospice nurse later in life but has always loved writing and reading. She holds a BA in English and a BSN from the University of Northern Colorado and attended school at University of Mississippi many years ago. T.C. loves cooking, traveling, outdoor activities, reading, and spending time with her family.

CPSIA information can be obtained
at www.ICGtesting.com
Printed in the USA
FFHW020637311218
50017371-54771FF

9 781643 009766